CONTENTS

	Acknowledgments	
1	Star Child	
2	Instinct	Pg.24
3	Water Woman	Pg.40
4	Down the Riverside	Pg.46
5	Amen	Pg.50
6	The Neighbours	Pg.54
7	The Post Office	Pg.67
8	Sacrifice	Pg.88
9	The Prophet	Pg.92
10	Scorpio's	Pg.97
11	Mount Fran	Pg.112
12	Seed	Pg.126

Acknowledgements:

Thank you to Almighty God for the talent. Thank you to my parents Bernard and Mary Georges, and my sister Jeanel, for always encouraging me to develop my skills. Thank you to my husband Dalton and our children Justin and Dominique for their love and support. Thank you to my editors, Dr. Bernard Frampton and Roy Sanford, cover illustrator Cherise Harris, and photographer Jason Carrington. Thank you to my dear Dominican childhood friends-(Saints you know who you are!), the English teachers of St. Martin School, the English literature teachers of Convent High School, the Waitukubuli Writers and Nature Isle Literary Festival, Kristopher Noseworthy, Sir.Tim, Patrick Pembo jr, Glenora, Stan and Nat, Francis J, and to all my friends and colleagues. God bless you all!

1. Star Child

Dunstan watched the girl in the white bikini as she stood at the water's edge.

She stretched her lithe arms as wide as a wingspan and turned her face up to the sun with closed eyes. She smiled broadly, seeming to revel in the perfect weather. She strode into the water, until the waves lapped her thighs. She dove, and broke the surface several feet away. He continued to observe her surreptitiously through his binoculars. There were other lovely girls on the beach this evening, but the swimmer stood out because of her pristine bikini and athletic figure.

Her arms moved like blades as she scythed through the water. She pulled away from the other swimmers with amazing speed. He turned his gaze and began scanning the beach from one end to the other, so as not to alert the suspicion of his wife who lay next to him.

He glanced down at her now from the corner of his eye. She was on her back, her middle-aged body discreetly clad in a black one piece suit. Behind her old Rayban shades, she seemed to be asleep. She had been a good policeman's wife, if not a bit too conservative for his liking. If she asked him outright about ogling the girl, he would have admitted it, still his guilty conscience made him keep up his pretense. He swept his binoculars over the beach so quickly the sun bathers blurred into multi-coloured dots, before he trained the glasses out to sea.

His wife made a sound in her throat and turned on her side muttering about the heat. He hastily pointed the glasses up at the sky and stared at some unremarkable sea birds lazily floating with the wind currents. He was amused by his own reaction.

He swung his glasses back to the water and stared at a young couple's passionate embrace. He looked for a few more minutes before searching out the swimmer but couldn't spot her. He tried to judge how far she could have gone. He scanned slower, from left to right, seeking her among the bathers who were further out. Nothing.

Puzzled, he lined up his sights with the horizon to scan downwards to the shore and then gave a sharp exclamation. She was out there, swimming backwards into the horizon. He was startled. It was impossible that she could have swum that far that fast. Yet as he watched she disappeared completely from view, not even his powerful glasses could pick her out anymore. He realized that he was ramming the viewer to his glasses, and that his wife was no longer asleep at the same time. She was looking at him with a disgust he could sense even through her shades.

"Now that should be illegal," she said and gestured with a quick jerk of her chin to the young couple in the passionate clinch. He grunted, keeping his gaze out to sea.

"Did you see that?" he asked suddenly and sat up straighter.

"See what?" she asked, taking off her shades.

"There was a flash of light, like a flare or something way out there," he pointed. She reached into her coat lying on a towel next to her and took out her glasses. She raised them to her eyes without putting them on. The strange light was fading away.

"Well, I don't know…" she said, "Maybe it's a signal from a boat?"

He shook his head and told her he had noticed a girl swimming in the same area. She pursed her lips and put her glasses down. In a sharp voice she suggested he might find a swim more productive than being a peeping tom, and lay with her back towards him.

Twenty-one years of marriage told him what that meant, but twenty-six years of policing told him something was up with the swimmer. He couldn't shake the feeling the girl was in trouble. The feeling grew stronger as the afternoon wore on. High tide came and the sun started to set. Still no sign of her.

Margery got up and started packing the remains of their picnic lunch. He washed the cutlery off in the sea and stood for a moment in a vain hope that the girl would reappear.

Other people, who preferred the cool of the sunset to swim, drove up and there was an exchange of bathers, as those who were there from earlier in the day began to wade back to shore.

"Dunstan…the kids are coming over tonight. Let's get going. I swear since you retired you move slower than ever." Margery said and began walking back to the car. She was now wearing a purple kaftan over her swimsuit.

They drove home in silence; the palm trees casting shadows over the one lane road while the pinkish hue of the sunset dissolved into the muted blue-grey of dusk. They had dinner with their children and grandchildren then went to bed.

During breakfast, Dunstan picked at his eggs without enthusiasm still feeling full from dinner. He drank his cocoa tea with relish however as Margery had made it with the extra nutmeg he enjoyed. Margery cleaned up the kitchen and started making preparations for lunch. She hummed along with a classic Nat King Cole song playing on the radio. The news came on, and the headlines made him stop his fork's meanderings.

The voice of the newsreader came across crisp and professional as he reported the finding of the body of a young woman at sea. Some fishermen had recovered the body and turned it over to authorities. The report ended. No name was given and no cause of death offered.

He stared at his congealed egg, deep in thought. Margery stopped washing dishes and sighed heavily. She wiped her hands on her apron and left the kitchen. When she returned, she handed him the cordless phone and returned to the sink without a word.
He smiled at her back, and dialed Leo.

Later that day, about noon, he sat in Leo's office, which had once been his office.

"Chief, it seems straight forward to me," Leo said and leaned back in his leather chair. Dunstan squirmed slightly in the straight back wood chair; uncomfortable being on this side of the desk.

"I don't think so Leo. There was an odd flash of light at the spot where she disappeared. Like an explosion or a flare. I can't explain it but she didn't just drown."

"Well the autopsy report will be on my desk tomorrow, but we have to inform her family first. Her parents, surname of Ford, live up Mount Fran. The road is barely motorable and their phone is disconnected."

Leo tapped his fingers on the desk twice, a sign the discussion was over.

Dunstan rose. "Who's doing the slicing?"

Leo stood up as well, "Dr. Lewis--the daughter--not the father. He's retired too."

Dunstan nodded as a plan formed in his mind, and took his leave. On his way out of the station, he was delayed several times by colleagues and former subordinates asking the same question: How's retirement going?

While Dunstan and Leo had been talking, Sergeant Charles and his partner took their time hiking up Mount Fran. The road had never been paved and the rocky path snaked its way up the mountain.

Sergeant Charles spotted a ripe hand of bananas on a tree close to the Ford's house. His partner Sergeant Aurelius, newly transferred from the country area, protested the theft to no avail. Charles ate one banana swiftly and put the hand on the ground at the base of the tree. He took several banana leaves that were already on the ground and covered the hand. He heard a sharp cough from his partner and straightened up to see a woman looking directly at him. She was about 60, sun-dried and wrinkled from the outdoors. From her heavily stained clothes and the threatening way she gripped her cutlass, he assumed she was the farmer.

"Get away!" She said and took a step forward.

Charles raised his hands in defense, "Mrs. Ford? Sorry about that. I was just hungry."

It took both officers some time to convince her they were not simply thieving trespassers, but eventually she allowed them into the house and introduced her husband.

Sergeant Aurelius gave them the news of their daughter's death.

"We know," Mr. Ford said simply.

He retrieved a folded sheet of paper from his jeans pocket and handed it to Sergeant Charles, before leading his wife out of the room. To the officers, she seemed so much smaller and older now than the cutlass wielding avenger in the banana field.

Aurelius read the letter over Charles's shoulder. It was warm and flowery, at odds with the down-to-earth farmers they had just met.

"Why did she sign it 'Star Child'?" Aurelius asked.

"Because that is what we called her," Mr. Ford said as he returned to the living room alone. He sat down on the old paisley covered couch with a stiffness that bespoke arthritis. Sergeant Charles made a motion to Aurelius who took out her notebook and began making notes.

Mr. Ford gazed out the window. Thin shafts of gold sunlight filtered through the rips in the jade green leaves of the banana plants and disappeared into the layers of mulch below. Charles and Aurelius exchanged glances as the silence lengthened.

"Mr. Ford, I know this is difficult for you…" Charles began.

"Annamarie was not our blood child," Mr. Ford interrupted abruptly. Aurelius resumed her scribbling.

"We found her after a storm in the field…it was such a bad storm. All the plants fall down flat. She was wrapped up in some kind of shiny cloth, kind of silver, kind of gold. It change color when you turn it to the light."

"You think she was abandoned in the storm?" Aurelius asked, her voice ringing with outrage. Sergeant Charles frowned at her but she ignored him.

Mr. Ford shook his head slightly, "I don't know. The cloth was waterproof and she was wrapped up all over, all her head and her body was covered so she wasn't wet when we found her. She was lucky, I thought it was some kind of evil somebody put for us. I almost hacked it with my cutlass, but then she started to cry."

Mr. Ford pinched the bridge of his nose with his thumb and index fingers.

"When she got big and wanted to know where she came from, we told her she came from the stars to us. She was our little star child." His voice broke.

The officers thanked him and took their leave.

It was raining when Dunstan rolled over in bed the next morning. He groaned as his temples pounded with the start of a migraine. It always happened after he had nightmares.
Not so much nightmares, as disturbing images. Images of a bikini clad bronze goddess diving into the sea and reaching the horizon with one tremendous backstroke; images of the sea exploding so only a crater was left, with the figure of a woman lying among the seaweed and flopping fish.

Margery was already up as usual, cooking breakfast and baking bread. She was also on the phone to someone. As he came barefoot down the stairs, he overheard part of the conversation.

"…just can't seem to relax and enjoy it. We've been waiting so long to have him as a real part of the family."

The emotion in her voice surprised him, made him pause before alerting her to his presence. He stood outside the partially open kitchen door. There was a pause as his wife listened to the other party on the line.

"That's what you think! I caught him looking at young girls on the beach on Sunday, and to think I'm the one who gave him that expensive viewer," Her voice rose in indignation.

Dunstan took a few steps back from the door and made a production of going into the living room and turning on the television. He sensed rather than heard Margery open back the kitchen door to take a look. He met her startled gaze as he walked back to the kitchen. The smell of fried codfish, onions and garlic assailed him as he walked past her.

She ended the call hurriedly and asked if he was feeling well. In twenty-one years, he had never turned on the T.V before seeking out breakfast. He took his plate and coffee and went to eat in front of the T.V, although he knew she didn't like it, but he was annoyed she had been talking about him.

As if by fate, the face of his bronze goddess smiled out at him from the top left corner over the announcer's shoulder. The autopsy ruled death by drowning; the police were treating it as a suicide. Case closed. The report continued with an account of allegations of doping made against her during the last Olympic Games.

It was as if the sun burst through a dark fog. Of course, he'd heard about it but he hadn't recognized her on the beach. The year of the Olympics he had been preoccupied trying to avoid personal scandal. His son, Xavier, had gotten caught with drugs. Dunstan had dipped into precious savings to hurriedly ship the boy off to the States.

He listened intently tapping his chin as the announcer related Annamarie's blistering time in the backstroke heats, and the subsequent accusation of steroid use. She refused to be tested and was banned.

"...Ford was one of several gifted athletes sponsored by EverGreen Labs, the American research facility based in St. Marts since the early 1900s. In a statement released just today, Ever Green Labs expressed its regret over Ford's death..."

Dunstan's hand stilled and he frowned. He exhaled and slumped back into the chair.

"And that is that," he muttered.

The news report ended with a shot of The Ford's house on Mount Fran. Apparently, they refused to speak to reporters. There was brief footage of Mrs. Ford flourishing a cutlass at the television crew. Despite his dark mood, he smiled watching the big, male reporter maintain a respectful distance.

The rain stopped after breakfast, and when Margery went outside to hang up clothes he joined her. The smell of the rich, wet earth was thick in the air, making him ache for days spent hiking in the forest. Before the promotion, he led a drug squad ambushing marijuana growers in the mountains. There were more murders per capita than the public realized. He knew of bodies found in boats in the island's waters. Locals and foreigners were caught up in the burgeoning cocaine trade. There were also bodies found in the forest, and buried by police, to save tax-payers the expense of funerals. Beneath its beautiful façade, St. Marts hid many secrets.

Now this beautiful, young girl.

He felt weary suddenly and for the first time since his retirement, glad not be in the middle of it. Yet he was probably the last person to see her alive, and he could not shake the sense of responsibility; especially if EverGreen Labs was involved.

He told Margery he was going for a drive and would be back for lunch. He dressed quickly, inhaling as he zipped up his pants. In just a few months, Margery's extra cooking and his inactivity were showing up on his waistline.

Dr. Ashla Lewis's office was empty, because her father's patients were wary of her youth. She had over forty years of her father's reputation to live up to.

"Yep, they're big shoes alright," she said with a smile in her American accent.

"People will get used to you. It's not like you're a foreigner," he offered by way of comfort.

She laughed. "I might as well be. I haven't been home in years, not even for vacation. It's so ironic I ended up back here…I always said it was too small for me." She was refreshingly self-deprecating, not like some of the other young graduates who came back to sit on their laurels.

"Unlike Annamarie, I used to hate it here," she added.

His interest perked up.

"You knew Annamarie Ford personally?"

"We became acquainted when we both got back a year ago. She was a nice girl, a little eccentric," Dr. Lewis responded, glancing at her phone. "She loved island life with a passion I couldn't understand. That and swimming," she continued, toying with the phone cord.

Dunstan spoke his thoughts out loud.

"It's ironic; an exceptional swimmer who dies from drowning."

"Umm," she agreed.

"Did you notice anything unusual about the body?" he asked.

She shot him a sharp glance. He noticed her easy smile seemed to falter.

"Nothing that would make me question my assessment of the cause of death. Look, I already had to convince the police chief that I was competent to do the autopsy, so I hope you're not here to question my abilities too?"

She quirked an eyebrow but he could see the amusement in her eyes.

"Not at all, I'm just here as an interested citizen," he reassured.

"Ah well that makes it easy, the findings were already made public, and the details aren't of interest to anyone. So I hope you've got an ache or pain somewhere for me to treat." She replied.

Dunstan's lids lowered as he studied her. She was lying.

"Ashla, what are you afraid of?" He asked bluntly.

Her smile disappeared and she stared at him in astonishment.

"Honestly Chief, it's not a question of fear, it's just the police asked me not to disclose details of the autopsy to anyone. I'm just trying to accommodate them."

She was discomfited and looked as though she wanted him to leave. At first, he had helped to relieve her boredom but now she was uncomfortable.

Still, she had known Dunstan since she was a child. He was the law in St. Marts and it was hard to shake the perception even though he was retired. She decided there was no harm in telling him.

"There is something about Annamarie that I think is a medical oddity, but it's got no bearing on her death, and it's certainly not something I'm afraid to share," she added. Dunstan remained pokerfaced.

"But you've got to keep it in confidence. Chief Leo doesn't want any more press on her than is necessary. He thinks the whole Olympic scandal thing was bad for tourism. I've tried to tell him that nobody else in the world cares but there's no reasoning with locals," she said in exasperation. She leaned in a few inches over the desk although there was no one around to hear them.

"There are two things that make the body a unique specimen: first, she was perfect in every way, and I do mean perfect. There was no sign of the usual deterioration of age, no illness; every organ was in mint condition," She revealed.

"And the second thing?" he prompted.

"Yes, besides the fact that the body shows no effects of age, pollution or else, she appears to have extra musculature in her arms," Ashla pointed to her own right shoulder and the back of her arm to elaborate.

"She had an extra length of muscle that ran from her shoulder to her wrist in both arms. It was the sort of thing that might have been missed even by a good doctor," She explained.

"Then how did you find it?"

"Well I was so compelled by the pristine nature of the body, I kept looking to find something- anything-wrong with it. I mean it's like she was perfect to begin with, and then enhanced." Ashla was obviously intrigued, but Dunstan was following the information to another conclusion.

"These extra muscles, triceps etc., would they account for her swimming ability?" he theorized. She pursed her lips and nodded slowly.

"It could... I suppose. Those muscles are certainly developed by swimming, but of course it doesn't account for how she got that way in the first place. This belongs in a medical journal, not shut up as an irrelevant asterix in an autopsy report." She sighed her frustration.

As Dunstan left the office, he turned to wave a final goodbye and caught Dr. Lewis lifting her phone for the umpteenth time. He smiled and spared a moment's pity for her. Her practice was only a few months old. It would take a while to convince her father's skeptical patients that she wasn't too young to know what she was doing.

He stopped off at the station as he was prone to do most afternoons to chat with the older officers. Leo didn't mind as these officers were doing mainly desk duty. They were glad to see Dunstan, to reminisce about the old days. Through a few careful questions, he found out about Sergeants Charles and Aurelius. It seemed the incident with the stolen bananas was still the running joke for the day. He decided to tackle Aurelius who would want to make a good impression.

She was collecting banana skins that had been piled on the desk she shared with Charles.

"Looks like a monkey party in here," Dunstan joked as he walked up to the desk. She rolled her eyes but recognized him and so did not retort. He introduced himself formally and asked her how she was finding the work. She shrugged slightly.

"It's different office politics, that's about it," she replied. He nodded.

Dunstan sat in Charles's chair and provided a sympathetic ear to the young officer. He learned that after Aurelius had told the banana story to the other officers and the practical jokes began, Charles had stuck her with all the paperwork.

"Oh really?" Dunstan interrupted her litany and picked up the top sheet of her immense pile. Fortunately, she was behind on her reports and so he found himself reading Mr. Ford's account of finding Annamarie as an abandoned baby. Casually, he picked up the next sheet; the so-called suicide note. He glanced over his glasses and saw Leo come out of his office for a stretch. He dropped the note, bent as though to pick it up but instead quickly crammed it into his jacket pocket. He straightened up and skimmed through the first sheet of Mr. Ford's story.

Leo scanned the room which unfortunately was relatively empty due to the lunch hour and spotted Dunstan almost immediately. Dunstan ignored him and continued to read quickly. A particular detail rang a bell but before he could figure it out, Leo was standing before him with an out-stretched right hand. Leo was respectful but firm as he escorted Dunstan out of the station. Dunstan waited until Leo went back inside, then got out of the car and returned to the station.

He breezed past the front desk with a hurried "forgot-my-keys" thrown over his shoulder to the officer on duty. He avoided the main office where Leo was lecturing the bewildered Sergeant Aurelius and went to the records office. Officer James, who was on the brink of retirement himself, showed him to one of the network computers hidden behind a wooden screen.

Satisfied that he could not be seen unless someone stepped from behind the partition, Dunstan sat at the computer. He crossed his fingers and typed in his password. It still worked. He spared a moment to be annoyed at the negligence of the tech staff.

He began with the 20-year-old records. He typed "abandoned child" in the search box and pulled up several records. He did a more detailed search using the phrase "gold cloth" and found one case: The Fords. He tapped his chin deep in thought and noticed his glasses were covered in fingerprints. He pulled them off and wiped them with the bottom edge of his polo shirt.

The station was small and soon somebody would come up to the second floor to look something up, or most likely check e-mail. He typed in "shiny cloth" and the case files went up to four. Four in thirty years: The first one was the Ford file, and then the others occurred at five year intervals. He stared uneasily at the screen. Why hadn't someone seen the pattern?

He went back to the 1950s and found the case that had triggered his memory. A Mr. Horace Wallis had found a child on his door step wrapped in some kind of flexible foil material. It had been one of the last cases Dunstan's father had worked on. Mr. Wallis had five children of his own but his wife had taken pity on the baby boy and raised him. He had grown up to be an exceptional runner, migrated to England and won many medals and records. Cedric Wallis, Dunstan remembered his name. Wallis retired from running just as he seemed to be in top form. He died while jogging. The other joggers said it looked like he was struck by a strange looking bolt of lightning, but the case was ruled a heart attack.

Dunstan frowned. He did not read science fiction stories and the current popular fantasy movies left him cold. He definitely did not appreciate the pattern unfolding on the screen. He took his search another five years forward. Another baby, actually a toddler, had been found by a Rastafarian. This child was naked, but was gripping a shiny swath of cloth in her hand. She seemed to have walked a distance from the state of her feet. The Rastafarian had not reported finding the child to the police. When she started school, she had no birth certificate to the horror of the principal. The details of her finding came out when the principal asked Child Welfare to investigate.

On an impulse Dunstan copied down her name and names of the last two children on the list. He really should go before he got caught but there was one more thing he had to check. He typed in "EverGreen Labs" in the search box. There were a few hits, but not nearly as many as there should have been. He noted the Lab was listed as a sponsor of the track star, Cedric Wallis. He signed out and left quickly

When he got home, Margery told him that a Sergeant Aurelius had called for him. He thanked her and ate his lunch in silence. After lunch, he lay on the macramé hammock in the verandah and tried to process what he had learnt. His bungalow home was near the street but few cars passed this way at this time. Most people were at work. He shifted uncomfortably in the hammock. The cool breeze was refreshing and he felt the tension begin to ease out of his mind and body. Margery sat on a wicker chair shelling peas and listening to the radio. A call-in program was on and amidst the usual complaints of potholes and poor customer service, someone called to talk about Annamarie Ford. Dunstan turned up the volume.

It was the steroid scandal brought up at last. A few others called, including a regular caller known as the Prophet. The show's host tried to be patient as the Prophet rambled on before he said something coherent, "...too many of us have gifts and never live up to our potential as the Almighty planned for us. Take the swimming girl for example, she just give up! Never take the test to prove she wasn't on the steroids. She just throw the gift away. She get punish for that." The host cut him off.

Dunstan drifted into a nap with the Prophet's words on his subconscious. Two gifted athletes, a swimmer and a runner...dead before the age of 30. So many coincidences...ok even he could not deny the design: Two abandoned babies wrapped in iridescent cloth ...adopted by farmers. Why were they always found in the bush? Why not in the town?

His uneasy thoughts moved to EverGreen Labs, or 'the Lab' as locals referred to it. That was a dead end. The Lab was as impenetrable as a diplomatic embassy; hallowed ground where no local authority could trespass. He recalled a couple of unsolved investigations that died at

EverGreen's massive gates. The judge denied his request for a search warrant without explanation. Then he received directives from the Commissioner's office, ordering him to re-direct resources to other matters.

Local gossips described The Lab as a strange place where strange things happened. He thought of Annamarie's peculiar musculature; one of the Lab's bizarre experiments?

The breeze raised goosebumps on his swarthy forearms. The problem with retirement was now there was too much time to think. He reflected on his capitulations over the years to political pressure. He had done his best to uphold the law but he knew he wasn't above reproach. He should have fought harder to investigate EverGreen Labs. He had let ambition compromise his integrity.

I'm ashamed, he admitted at last. Her death was ultimately his fault.

The evening wore on and Margery rose to turn on the lights. She exclaimed in irritation because the power was out again; the second time for the week. She ran quickly to light candles and put batteries in the biggest hurricane flashlight before all the daylight disappeared. They sat on the verandah looking at the flicker of lights in their neighborhood as people came out on their porches, to escape the stuffiness inside the houses. It was nice. Some of the neighbors were moving from house to house to say goodnight and enjoy the unexpected community spirit.

Dunstan told Margery he was going to the bathroom and took one of the candles with him. He paused at the phone and took his list out of his pockets. Margery was talking to one of the wandering neighbors; Mrs. Greer, the gossip. She'd stay awhile.

He looked at the name of the Rastafarian girl and hoped she had not married, because that would make his search more complicated. He thumbed through the phone book, and unexpectedly came across the father's name. That was a surprise.

The phone rang a long time before a rough voice answered.

" 'Lo?"

"Mr. Welsh? This is Chief George calling."

There was a silence and a muttering. The voice became hostile.

"Yah, I remember you. Take out my good field a while back."

Dunstan blinked; a complication he should have foreseen.
"Well, that's a long time ago," he replied.

There was an even more hostile silence. Dunstan decided to ask his question before the other man hung up.

"I'm looking for your daughter Mr. Welsh, Queen Sheba."

"Queen Sheba is not your business Mr. Policeman. She is beyond the reach of Babylon,"

Dunstan felt a sense of dread.

"I am sorry sir. Could you tell me if she was good at sports?"

As belligerent as Welsh was, he could not hide his pride.

"She was good man, real good. She could see clear across the miles. Best in dem bow and arrow games."

"She was an archer then…" Dunstan mused. Welsh, still caught up in his memories confirmed it.

"She get a scholarship from the Americans, but she don't stay long in the devil system. She come home, start to build a house on my land, put in the phone, and pipe water. She was a real nice child," his voice trailed off.

"How did she die?" Dunstan softened his voice, but Welsh had had enough and after calling down Jah's vengeance on all policemen, he hung up. Dunstan put the phone down and returned to the verandah where Mrs.

Greer was still talking away. The power came back on and he and Margery went to bed.

Early on Friday morning he tracked down the last two names on his list. He didn't call but just found out where they lived. As he suspected, they lived in very rural areas, enjoying the best of fresh air and food. They were both boys; aged 15 and 10.

James and Carl, he said their names over and over in his head. He felt a sense of urgency about them. They were under threat in some way. He ate his breakfast of fried plantains under Margery's watchful eye. He broke out of his reverie to thank her for the meal.

Dunstan went to the living room, although the sun always shone too brightly there in the mornings for his comfort. He moved some furniture around, earning a sharp rebuke from Margery. He told her he'd fix everything back and moved an armchair to the corner furthest away from the window. He opened the newspaper and went to the sports section. It would become the first thing he would do after breakfast in the years that followed.

He took a crumpled piece of paper from his pocket. The edges were becoming gray from handling. He smoothed it out and read Annamarie Ford's last message to her parents.

Dear Mum and Dad, don't be sad because I've failed. I appreciate and love you with all my heart and spirit. I am living beyond my appointed time. My only crime is loving this home and this life too well, but the gods punish those who spurn their gifts. So I shine bright and brief, Love your Star Child.

He read it again and tapped his stubbled chin.

She'd known she was going to die, but there was nothing to indicate suicide.

"The "gods" punish those who spurn their gifts…" he muttered. He thought he understood at last, as incredible as it seemed.

There was a message here, but this was not a suicide note.

He glanced up as Margery came into the room. She was followed by Leo. She left them without a word.

Dunstan was not surprised to see him and handed him the note.

Leo's light skin flushed.

"You put me in a difficult position Dunstan; I have to ask you not to come to the station again. I feel you abused our friendship and took advantage of your influence." Leo's voice rose.

"Leave police business to the police!" he insisted. He turned to go.

"She didn't drown herself," Dunstan said. Leo hesitated then turned back.

"What? How do you know that?" Leo asked. His eyes narrowed.

Dunstan indicated to the letter Leo held.

"She loved life. She loved her parents. She tried to prepare them. She knew she was going to die. Somehow, somebody killed her."

It seemed to him that Leo's face paled, the flushed hues drained away.

"Chief, she was sponsored for the Olympics by EverGreen Labs. You must know that?"

Dunstan nodded, his face grim.

"I believe they experimented on her, and when she didn't, or wouldn't continue to compete, they killed her," he said. It sounded even more insane spoken aloud. Leo was going to think he had gone senile.

But Leo's enraged reaction shocked him.

"You were Chief of Police for eleven years. Don't play dumb with me! You know how this works. We keep order and we follow directives. The

Lab is off limits. I don't care what kind of deal they have with Government, I'm not risking my career for it!"

At first Dunstan gaped, stunned. He stood and glared up at Leo.

"They killed Annamarie Ford, and possibly other athletes going all the way back to the 1950s. They're going to do it again. Where's the justice?"

He restrained himself from grabbing Leo by the collar.

"You had your chance and you did nothing. The investigation is over!" Leo shot back.

They stared at each other in tense silence.

Dunstan felt his own anger slowly dissolve into despair. Leo had been his protégé and was simply following the example set.

Dunstan exhaled, and offered his hand to Leo.

He forced himself to speak in a lighter tone, "I'm thinking of joining the National Sports Board to keep myself occupied"

Leo took his hand quickly and squeezed it. He smiled in obvious relief.

"That's a good thing Chief. You'd be good as a mentor, you were to me. I can see you helping the youth to achieve their potential." He replied, oblivious to the irony.

Leo left with the air of a man rid of a troublesome problem.

Exactly one week after Annamarie Ford had opened her arms for a final time to the wind, Dunstan and Margery lay in their favourite spots on the beach. It was a gray day and the wind made the sea choppy. He was glad to think that she had had that perfect day to enjoy. He thought of her with sad affection; poor, blessed yet blighted child.

Margery signaled that she wanted more Hawaiian Tropic smeared on her back and rolled back onto her stomach. She lay with her eyes closed and her Rayban shades askew.

"So...did you find out what really happened to that girl?" she asked drowsily. He gave a start as though she had read his thoughts. He looked down at her. So she had known all along what he was up to. He smiled with admiration for his quiet, clever wife.

He had not used the binoculars today, now he picked them up and trained them on the horizon and scanned down to the shoreline.

"It wasn't suicide," he said.

She sighed.

He watched the swimmers, especially the children, looking for some spark of genius.

"I think the Sports Board is a good idea. Lots of kids need something to aspire to, with all this drugs business," she commented.

He did something now that he had never done during his career.

"I'm afraid I'll never be able to prove she was murdered," he confided.

They were silent for a few minutes. The gulls screeched overhead.

"You'll never stop trying. You too stubborn to give up," she said.

He leaned over and kissed her oily right shoulder.

He was distracted by loud splashing, and looked to see one young lad turning summersaults in the water. It made Dunstan think of the other two names on his list; two boys aged 15 and 10 years-old.

No doubt they were already exceptional athletes, earmarked for EverGreen Labs' patronage, but very soon they would come to the attention of the National Sports Board, and he would be there waiting for them.

He must find a way to save them, and the others to come: Those Star Children.

2. Instinct

Uneasy, Claudian watched her son play on the jungle gym. Ronnie seemed so much smaller and vulnerable, compared to the other children. When the boy at the top of the jungle gym playfully kicked at Ronnie's hands as he struggled up, she felt her breath catch. Ronnie gave a bleat but continued to pull himself up. She smiled at his determination. He beamed back- proud of his little achievement.

It was a beautiful day. A cool wind wafted through the new playground, cooling many fevered little brows. It was a small play area: two swing sets, a sandbox, some slides. Nothing too fancy, but it was more than the children of the town of St. Frances had ever had. There was even a young guard on duty, although she doubted he could manage the local thugs who were bound to come once it got dark. She felt sorry for him as she watched him pick at a bandage on his chin. He would probably end up calling the police for help.

She sighed, enjoying the combination of warm sunshine and refreshing breezes. The moist grass was emerald green and the clouds looked like cotton in the turquoise sky. She inhaled and took in the scents from all directions: The damp, rich earth, the hibiscus flower bushes, the sweat of the children, the Chanel no. 5 on the grandmother on the next bench, the blood of the cut on the guard's chin. She exhaled a sharp breath and closed her eyes briefly.

Always overdoing it, she chided herself. She opened her eyes to see the grandmother on the next bench was staring at her. She was used to that. She tried to appear casual. It was always harder to restrain herself outdoors.

Claudian glanced at the jungle gym. Ronnie was no longer there. She stood up and scanned the park, looking for his red T-shirt. She swallowed hard and sprinted over to the jungle gym trying not to let panic dictate her movements. She picked up his scent and followed it to the trees on the outskirt of the park. There was no boundary between the park and woods; the trees just grew denser.

Once she was out of view of the other people in the park, she dropped to all fours quickly and the hair on the back of her neck stood up. She sniffed the air; nostrils flared. Ronnie was a short distance away. She could also smell that another boy was with him. The boy was chasing Ronnie deeper into the woods. A growl escaped her before she could control it and she ran hunched over from the waist. They were just yards away, flashing in and out of her view between trees. Ronnie's shrill screams drove her mad and, running full tilt, she slammed into the bigger boy from the back. He went flying and landed unconscious on the ground. He never saw her coming. Ronnie stood a few feet away, wary of her in her present state.

"We were just playing hide and seek mum, Keith was trying to catch me," he complained.

Claudian was appalled. The other boy was only about six or seven, just tall for his age. And she had bowled him over like a rampaging bull.

I am an animal, she thought with dismay.

Ronnie was upset at having to leave early, and whined until she wanted to scream with irritation. She tried not to think of how Keith's mother had reacted, when she carried him back to the playground. Keith had woken up but was very confused. He told his mother he had tripped much to Claudian's relief. Claudian glanced in her rear view mirror and saw the ambulance pulling up to the park entrance. She slumped down in her seat and sharply lectured Ronnie about running off.

Because it was Sunday, Claudian and her husband had dinner with her in-laws. She liked her mother-in-law very much but her father-in-law made her uncomfortable. She could feel his eyes on her at all times; as though he thought she might steal the silverware. The dinner was delicious although the steak was a little too well done for her taste.

"Ronnie how is pre-school?" her mother-in-law Margery asked, smiling at Ronnie.

"He's doing really well at his numbers and knows his alphabet," Claudian responded warmly.

"Oh that's wonderful!" Margery replied.

Claudian's husband, Xavier, shrugged his shoulders and smiled.

"Yeah, he's a little nerd, can't play sports to save his life."

His father grunted.

"The boy is too puny. He's going to get knocked down all the time."

"Dunstan," Margery reproached.

Ronnie stared at his grandfather with his mouth slightly agape.

Xavier laughed. "We got to get him in the gym Dad, and start building him up for soccer."

Claudian could not participate in the teasing. She knew there was an unspoken accusation that it was her fault Ronnie was small. It was her fault he was born premature; that her body had treated the unborn child like a virus and expelled it two months before her due date. Ronnie had to be sent overseas, and they still owed the clinic thousands of U.S. dollars. She bowed her head and wrung the blue and white striped napkin in her lap. Xavier's hand covered hers and he squeezed it. She blinked back sudden tears.

They said goodbye; Dunstan kissed her cheek without actually touching her. He smelled of the sea and suspicion.

Xavier backed his Lexus out of the driveway into the main road without looking. As he drove, she stared at his profile. He was so strong, confident and handsome. She was still amazed that he had wanted her.

"Stop staring at me girl," his teeth flashed white in the night. She giggled and put her head on his shoulder. He affectionately held her ponytail in his free hand as he steered effortlessly with his right hand. He ruffled the thick hair on the back of her neck hidden by her high collar, "How's my puppy doing?"

She stiffened, "Don't say that."

She flopped back into her own seat swept away by bitter memories. She flinched, seeing in her mind's eye the ring of children that hemmed her in at school. Every day they had thrown sticks and rocks at her as they shouted, "Bark, dog-girl, bark!" She felt a hot teardrop roll down her cheek.

Xavier already seemed to be deep in thought about something else. Probably work. She knew he was setting up an offshore bank with some businessmen from the U.S. There was a lot of red tape and bureaucracy involved. She didn't know how it all worked, neither did she care. There always seemed to be money when they needed it. They arrived home and Xavier collected Ronnie who was asleep, from the back seat.

Ronnie woke up as they entered the house and demanded to stay up a little longer.

"I'm not sleepy anymore," he pouted and crossed his thin arms across his chest. Xavier tickled him until he begged for mercy and they both ran upstairs laughing. Claudian followed and then stood watching them from Ronnie's bedroom door. How amazing to be so happy after all the years of despair. She left Xavier reading Ronnie his favorite story and went to the master bedroom.

She loved the feel of the plush carpet under her feet as she walked across the room to draw the curtains. She stood with the curtains in either hand looking at the view. The town lay to the west of them; pinpoints of light interspersed by areas of dark. Each dark area represented trees, or neighborhoods without electricity. Black outs were common these days for some unknown reason. Past the town lay the ocean. It flowed like a silken, black ribbon around the island. Far out to the horizon she could see the lights of the cruise ships as they sailed to the next port. It was one of the best views on Morn Fran. Well they did have one of the few mansions there after all. The rest of the land was owned by farmers, or the Lab.

She closed the curtains as Xavier strode into the room laughing. He tracked dirt on the navy carpet heedlessly and threw himself onto the bed with a loud exhalation. She winced at the sight of the footprints, imagining the look on Jessica's face the next day. Jessica was their housekeeper; an aggressive woman who could barely contain her contempt of Claudian. She was well paid or she would have gladly quit a long time ago. Her resentment was evident in the vigour with which she attacked her cleaning. Claudian resolved to clean the muddy prints as soon as Xavier left in the morning.

He was talking to her about how cute Ronnie was, something he had said about the story Xavier had read to him. Claudian nodded absently as she changed out of her clothes. They were designer made but Xavier complained they were also very ugly. He lay on his back watching her change.

"You've got a good body Clauds, why you always hiding it?" He teased. She did not answer as this had become a rhetorical argument. She stared at herself in her red lace bra and panties in the full-length mirror next to the French vanity. Yes, she did have a good figure. She also had broad shoulders, elfin ears and a thick line of hair that ran down her back. The hair was thickest on the back of her neck, like a scruff.

In the reflection of the mirror, she saw Xavier get off the bed and strip down as well. His back muscles rippled as he bent, took off his shoes and flung them carelessly to the bedroom door; more mud on the carpet.

They slept late the next morning and it was the sounds of Jessica vacuuming that finally woke them up. Xavier bounced out of bed with his usual energy and swatted her on the behind to get her up. Claudian groaned and tried to bury herself deeper into the sheets. She snatched a few more minutes as he showered and then roused herself when he came back into the room. He was on his cell having a one-sided conversation. The caller was doing all the talking, which was strange.

A loud knock at the bedroom door made her sit upright and cover herself. Xavier opened the door with his ear still glued to the phone. He gave a quick nod to the housekeeper's greeting and went back into the bathroom. Too late, Claudian remembered the muddy footprints as Jessica's steely glare burnt a path over the carpet. She stabbed Claudian with an accusing look and left abruptly. She returned with the vacuum.

Jessica did not say good morning to Claudian.

After breakfast, Claudian took Ronnie to visit her mother. He whined all the way during the drive to the church.

"I don't want to go by granny, she's always telling me what to do," he complained. She smiled.

"Granny tells me what to do too," she replied.

She parked and went through the church to the large house at the back. She resisted a shudder as the eyes of the stone saints pierced her; looking for a soul. Ronnie became quiet as usual when passing through the rows of statues and candles.

Claudian's mother, Maureen, was in the bishop's house, in the kitchen overseeing the menu for lunch. Besides organizing meals, her mother looked after the priests' robes for mass, the decorating and cleaning of the church, and the hiring of groundskeepers and other staff. It was a place of honor that she had earned through steadfast fanaticism.

"Claudian, child, why are you here without a head covering?" her mother asked scandalized.

Claudian's hands flew to her ears.

"My ponytail covers my ears mum," She murmured. Her mother was not impressed.

"You should know better than to go around like that. What would people say?"

Maureen turned her back in disapproval and resumed her discussion with the cook.

Claudian waited, standing uncomfortably to one side of the massive kitchen and away from the bay windows. Ronnie stood next to her gripping her hand and not complaining for once. His big brown eyes took in everything. The cooking staff bustled around preparing lunch and took no notice of them. Or so it seemed. More than once she caught the eyes of a cook staring at her curiously.

Probably wondering if I have a tail, she thought.

When Maureen finished issuing orders, she took them down a little pathway through the extensive grounds. It had the most manicured lawn that Claudian had ever seen and some very exotic flowers that were not native to St. Marts. They reached the cottage where Maureen lived. It was white with green trim, very neat and prim. Rose bushes surrounded it but there were only a few in bloom. Ronnie had once said it looked like the cottage in his storybook, where the wicked witch lived. She had tried hard not to laugh.

Maureen put a small plate of digestive biscuits on the overcrowded coffee table. Porcelain figurines and other knick-knacks fought for space in every inch of the cottage. She hummed "How Great Thou Art" as she poured out four cups of orange juice. Ronnie was staring at Maureen's portraits of the Sacred Heart of Jesus. Our Lord was depicted with his heart revealed in flames and staked with a cross. Claudian had been told that she must not look into His face because of her shame and sin.

Maureen launched into the usual series of lectures that passed for conversation between them.

"I can't understand how you could come into the presbytery without a hat, Claudian. It's as though you want everybody to pay attention to you or something," she muttered under her breath and sighed, "Our Lord knows I have borne this burden with steadfastness. We must all pay for our sins…I notice you weren't at Mass on Sunday."

Claudian knew her mother was not expecting answers so she continued to sip her juice.

Ronnie piped up unexpectedly.

"Daddy says Mass is for foolish people who believe in superstition."

The look on Maureen's face was priceless. She took a deep, indignant breath. Claudian held Ronnie's hand and gently told him that sometimes Daddy said things to be funny. Maureen was in awe of Xavier's good looks and family name but she strongly disapproved of his agnostic views.

Claudian remembered her mother's incredulity when they had announced their engagement. After all, what would a boy like that see in her freakish daughter? Maureen had been so shocked she had blurted out, "My sin is forgiven!"

The sin of birthing an imperfect child... Claudian thought as she sipped the overly-sweet juice.

Another memory came to her: Maureen coming into the Labour ward after Ronnie was born, and stripping him of his blanket, inspecting him, looking for flaws. The small patch of hair above his bottom made her catch her breath. The doctor took pity on her stricken face and told her it would go away eventually. Claudian did not bother to tell her that it had not.

Claudian looked at her watch and saw her obligatory hour was up. She rose and took Ronnie's sticky biscuit covered hand in hers. Claudian walked out the cottage, passing her father who was seated next to the door. A stroke had robbed him of his speech, and the power he used to wield over them in his drunken rages.

Xavier called her cell phone as she drove home. He sounded irritated and distracted. "I can't come for lunch. I've got meetings all day," he said.

She was disappointed, as the prospect of a long, lonely afternoon loomed. He swore at another call that came in from his office and he put her on hold. It took her a few seconds to realize that he had put her on conference call by mistake, but before she could alert him he began arguing with the other party.

"What do you want me to do? It's over. The sector is being shut down and investigated."

"We have an agreement," said a man with an American accent. Xavier swore again.

"Did you hear what I just said? It's over! Cut your losses."

The other man was calm, "We are very disappointed in you."

Claudian shivered at the fear in Xavier's voice. She had never heard him like this before. She quickly hung up, dropped the phone into her purse and sped home.

The afternoon turned to evening and she struggled to make sense of what she had overheard. Obviously Xavier was in trouble again. How crushed his parents would be if they knew. She stared at the elegant décor of her sitting room. How much of this was really hers? Did the house even belong to them? She put her hands to her face and dragged them slowly down her neck. Somehow, this must be her fault. Maybe in his eagerness to give her this lifestyle, he had fallen in with criminals.

She thought about Ronnie and what life would be like without private school and the status of being a rich man's son.

What if Xavier went to jail?

"What would the neighbors say?" she said out loud, and laughed without humor. She sounded like her mother.

She could hear Ronnie playing a video game upstairs. He was so good at playing by himself, her sweet, little boy. She felt the sting of tears starting and closed her eyes tightly. Exhausted from the worry, she slipped into an uneasy doze and dreamt her father was shaking her by the scruff. He was yelling at her and his breath smelled of stale rum.

"Claudian wake up," Xavier was shaking her shoulder. She sat up abruptly. He was switching on the lamp next to the sofa because it was now evening. How long had she slept?

"Ronnie!" she sat up with alarm.

"He's fine. He got some cocoa pebbles from the fridge and is eating them. Is this how you look after him? What have you been doing all day anyway?" Xavier's handsome face was stressed with deep, frown lines in his forehead.

She couldn't find the words to respond.

He went through the house turning on the lights and muttering under his breath. She lay for a few minutes on the couch in misery. Then her ears twitched at the sound of footsteps; two heavy footfalls and one light one, coming up the driveway. Had Xavier had invited people over? It seemed like the wrong night for guests.

She stood up and went upstairs to change into something more appropriate, passing Ronnie in the games room on her way. In the master bedroom, Xavier was lying across the bed with one arm thrown across his face. He appeared to be napping. She changed into a high collar, navy blue dress and went to the closet to look for some low heels.

The intercom beeped. Xavier started out of his doze violently. He swore as he rolled to his right and flipped the switch near the bed head.

"Who is it?" he barked.

"Is me, Jessica, sir."

Claudian's head jerked up with unpleasant surprise. Xavier rubbed his left eye with the ball of his hand.

"What is it?"

"I need to talk to you, sir, about a private matter. It's urgent." Jessica was being uncharacteristically humble.

Claudian went to the windows overlooking the driveway. Jessica and two men were standing at the gates. A first inkling that something was wrong began to grow. One of the men looked up and saw her. She didn't recognize him.

"Xavier…" she said quietly and moved away from the window.

He held up a finger as he spoke into the intercom, "This is a bad time Jessica, we'll speak tomorrow."

"Yes sir."

Claudian went back to the window standing to the side out of the line of sight. As she suspected Jessica did not go away but instead began punching the code for the gate on the keypad.

"Xavier there are men coming in!" she exclaimed. He jumped up and joined her at the window. The gates swung open and the men began a brisk jog up to the house. Xavier drew the drapes sharply and ran out of the room. He came back quickly with Ronnie tucked under his arm and practically threw the boy at her.

"Stay here, I'll deal with this!"

He ran into the adjoining bathroom and came out with a gun in his right hand. He checked the chamber and grabbed his jacket off the bed. He tucked the weapon into his belt behind him and put on the jacket. Claudian sat down heavily on the bed in shock with Ronnie grabbing her around the waist. Xavier left the room with a sharp warning to keep the door locked and blocked.

"Xavier," she whispered as the reality of what was happening sank in.

Ronnie's arms were locked around her so tightly she could barely breathe. She pushed him to the floor and ran to the door, unlocked it and peaked. Through the rungs of the balcony she could see Xavier in the foyer waiting.

Call the police! Her brain engaged suddenly.

But it was too late.

The front door was opened casually as though the homeowner was returning. Jessica's key no doubt. The men came in and faced Xavier. He spoke to them with arrogant authority he did not feel. She could smell his fear and sweat. The men took a step towards him and he drew his gun. They stopped. Again he ordered them to leave. No one moved.

Suddenly they both tackled him and the gun went off. She shut the door quickly, locked it and turned off the bedroom light. She whispered to Ronnie to get under the bed. His eyes were orange in the dark.

She rolled under the bed with him shaking and trying to quell the urge to scream. Downstairs she could hear all too acutely the sounds of Xavier getting the life beaten out of him. Ronnie whimpered and made a strange sound in his throat. She had never noticed before how his eyes glowed in the dark.

The men were asking Xavier about them, wanting to know where his weird wife and the kid were. Then loud, hard footsteps could be heard as someone ran up the stairs.

Ronnie whispered in a husky voice, "We have to help daddy, mummy! We have to help him!"

She cried then, covering her mouth with her hand. Convulsions shook her body. She prayed because there was no one else to save them. Then someone was at her bedroom door. She grabbed Ronnie, crushing him to her.

"Open up!" The man pounded on the door and started to kick it in.

They'll hurt Ronnie, they'll hurt him, they'll kill him, they'll hurt him....

She felt the bones in her back snap as she rolled out from under the bed. Agony coursed through her as her spine arched upwards and reshaped. Her neck popped and crackled as it broke and knit back, the scruff on her neck stood up straight. She was on her hands and knees, her toenails and fingernails clawed into the carpet and blood ran from her hands. Her jaw stretched to an unnatural angle and her gums ached as her teeth grew. All her senses screamed alert. From a distance, she could hear Ronnie wailing.

The door crashed open, and a stocky man dressed in jeans and a black T-shirt came in. He pulled up short.

"What...?" He whispered in horror.

In the dark room all he could see were four animal eyes glowing in the dark. A snarl made him jump and he raised a knife.

Claudian leapt on him then and ripped open his forearm while Ronnie attacked his calf. The man screamed and in his panic tore his arm out of Claudian's jaws, and fled the room. Claudian pursued him as he ran for the staircase. He tripped at the top of the stairs and rolled headlong down the long flight. He landed in a heap then scrambled to his feet holding his rib cage, and ran out the front door. The other man, who had been beating Xavier in the foyer, looked up startled. Growling, Claudian stood at the top of the staircase. The hallway light was on and he could see her fully. He stared up at her, his face transfixed with terror.

She lowered her head and tensed her haunches for the spring.

Suddenly, there was a gun-shot, and the man crumpled to the floor. Xavier painfully stood to his feet with his gun still trained on the man who did not move. Xavier studied the man's body for a minute, and then seeming satisfied, turned and hobbled to the staircase. He held on to the railing and painfully began to ascend. She backed up as he approached.

"Clauds," Xavier said softly. He was bloody and his eyes swollen, almost shut. He was breathing heavily out of his mouth because his lips were split. He wasn't handsome anymore. She growled in warning. He was now at the top of the landing and she had backed up even more into the hallway. He stared through the swollen slits of his eyes and she could see he was amazed. Not afraid, just amazed.

"That's my girl," he said, trying to smile.

Claudian snarled. Her human brain was outraged by his callous amusement. He had brought this danger on her and Ronnie. And he dared patronize her like some kind of pet?

She tensed her haunches and lowered her head with deadly intent but before she could do anything Ronnie scooted past her and stood between them, and the sight of him stopped her cold.

What in the name of the saints…?

He looked like a cross between a wolf and a boy: canine features, a snout and fangs. He was now hairy and lithe, and on all fours like she was. He had claws. Claws!

She was flooded with such acute sorrow that it took away the rage. What curse had she passed on to her baby?

Ronnie sat on his haunches, and panted. Xavier staggered to his son's side and sank wearily to the floor. He began to stroke the boy's pelt. Ronnie relaxed under the soothing strokes and before their eyes, he began to change. In a matter of minutes he was just a tired, little boy lying on the floor next to his father. Xavier put the gun on the floor, pulled out his cell phone and called the police.

Claudian watched him. He had kept a gun in the house all this time? She wanted to ask him why he hadn't told her, but her canine mouth could not form words. She was calmer now but unlike Ronnie, she did not seem to be able to change back. Xavier pulled Ronnie towards him and across his lap. The boy was deep in sleep.

"I love you, Claudian, I know you never believed it but I do…" Xavier spoke in a hoarse whisper.

He winced from pain and touched his swelling lips gingerly with a finger. Claudian lowered her head to the ground and stretched out her front legs. She tried not to look at them. Xavier was still talking but it was hard to follow. She wanted to be outside. The close confines of the house were beginning to affect her.

"I'm going to take Ronnie to my parents. It'll be ok. Those men want me, not you or Ronnie. I'm going back to Brooklyn to handle this."

She felt the bottom drop out of her stomach. She whined. He stroked Ronnie's back.

"Those guys aren't the ones I'm afraid of. It's the other ones, the ones who want you…can you understand me? They're coming for you now," He leaned forward to stare at her earnestly, and she sensed the truth in his tone.

He coughed. From a far distance Claudian could hear the sounds of sirens. She stirred restlessly, the urge to be outdoors was becoming stronger and Xavier's words were losing meaning. But she was not afraid. She was strong and powerful at last.

Xavier gestured to the back of the house where the mountain loomed.

"You have to go…go up into the bush and stay hidden. Get away from the Lab. I don't know if you were born like this or if those crazy doctors did this to you...but they've been waiting for this," he gestured to her changed body.

"My little problem worked to their advantage. They're watching us right now."

He nodded towards the ceiling. Claudian's eyes followed his to the light fixtures. She could not see the cameras and could no longer understand him in any case. The sirens were at the gates now.

"When they found out we were dating, they paid me to marry you to keep you close…gave us the house, the car."

He put out his hand towards her but she growled. He let his arm drop.

His words slurred, and he breathed out of his spoiled mouth heavily before he continued.

"They're coming for you, Clauds."

Claudian rose, the need to run was overpowering. She padded up to Xavier and sniffed Ronnie whose eyes flew open. They communed silently. She was not afraid for him anymore, since, after all, this was the nature of things; the young must go their own way. One day, instinct would bring them together again.

She took off down the stairs without a backward glance at Xavier, and ran through the open front door just as the police cars were pulling up. Ignoring the startled shouts, she bolted to the back of the house, through the brush and into the safe depths of the mountain.

3. Water Woman
For Toni

He could never get used to the way she ate raw fish.
It made his stomach turn, even after all their years together, to see her snap the head off and pop it still dripping gore into her mouth. Her strong teeth cracked the bones with ease as she chewed. It was just so…animal like.

They ate privately, the five of them huddled around a table he made from nailing together two broken crates. He had put fishnet over the windows to act as curtains to keep the curious from peeking in, although it had been years since anyone had bothered them. The children ate like she did, but he insisted that she partially cook their fish. They probably would have preferred it raw but he didn't care; they were going to act normal as long as he was head of the family.

She made a pretense of washing dishes in the large basin she had filled with river water. He watched her as she did this automatically; wash a plate and turn it over to dry in a small plastic dish-drainer. All the while, she stared out the window, watching the sea rush up to the shore and then retreat. She stared at the sea while her hands dipped plates and enamel cups. Then it was the cast iron pot she had cooked rice in, then a long handle spoon; all washed without her ever looking at her task.

He sighed. She stood with her back to him; her jet-black, long locks tied with some string at the nape of her neck and allowed to flow to her thighs. When he held her, her hair smelled of the sea and the coconut oil concoction she used as a hair dressing. She was still beautiful at almost 37, with bewitching silk, ebony skin and fiery eyes. She smiled without showing the full length of her teeth, so men stared at her full, curved lips and were lost. Her magic worked on him too. He would not admit to himself how desperately he still needed her.

She stared transfixed at the sea.
"I'm going for a swim," she suddenly said in her deep voice. She sounded rough with desire. He instantly put aside the net he had been trying to repair and got up from the grass mat.

"It's too late for that now," he said putting his arms around her, and physically lifted her away from the window. He placed her gently on the cot they shared, and spoke softly to her. He told her about the house they were going to have one day, with the big backyard and the swimming pool. He had been saying that for years. Her eyes were wet, and after a while she shut them so she would not have to look at him. He talked until he was dry in the mouth. She turned her back to him and dozed.

By the time dusk fell she was better. She washed clothes, and made him some hot bush tea to drink before the neighbor sailed up to collect him. He kissed her and she smiled, but her eyes were cold.

He waded out to his fishing partner and dropped his gear in the bottom of the boat. The old man grunted a greeting and packed the net away carefully under his seat. The children swam and frolicked around the boat with utter abandon. He laughed as they teased the old man, splashing him with water. Even the two-year-old could swim and dive perfectly. They waved and shouted their goodbyes. He gave each one a pat and told them to look after their mother. His eldest, a girl, looked at him quizzically with her slanted eyes so like her mother's. He felt uncomfortable under her scrutiny and signaled to the old man to go.

In his absence, she had nothing to do but to sit and remember. The children were self-sufficient, made so by force, because she had not been of use to them for so long. The older ones made tea for themselves and the younger ones, and put themselves to bed. They took turns watching her through the night. She tried not to be resentful of their care, and reminded herself that she must get over her illness and be a better mother.

When did this strange sickness come over her? One minute she had been happy-- no, not happy-- but at least content with her life, then suddenly one day she had woken up with an consuming desire to get away. She was a prisoner, trapped in a life that was of her own making. The abject poverty they lived in suffocated her with its unrelenting, intense minute-by-minute struggle to survive. The only thing that might have made this life bearable was the sea, and she had promised never to go back there.

Just before dawn, the children woke up and ate the fish she had saved from their supper. They ate it with sea grapes and crackers, chattering loudly and excitedly about their plans for the day. She felt old and tired listening to them, but something about their joy was infectious. They teased her until they coaxed a real smile from her, and they dragged her off to the river to play.

Their bodies, streamlined and sleek like otters, twined and tumbled over each other as they boisterously swam and dove off the river rocks. She shivered in the crisp coldness at first, her body slower to acclimatize than theirs. Eventually she slipped away to glean for fruits, awkwardly trying to climb trees to steal their booty. The sun became too hot for her and she began to feel faint. The sun's rays filtered through the leaves in thin streams seeking to sting her skin as she perched in the branches. Her mind wandered as she stared at the beams of light...

It had been his flashlight dancing on the surface of the water above that attracted her. The light was something new, shiny and tantalizing, drawing her up to the boat. He was not so interesting, but his treasures from the land acted like a magnet, and so she kept returning to the boat night after night.

Her magic ensnared him. She was so full of life and laughter. So he too returned night after night, with trinkets and flowers and shiny, cheap things he could ill afford. She had been eager to see the place where these fascinating items were from, but was afraid. Eventually he had coaxed her into the boat, and the rest...was many years ago.

She was drying out, sitting in this tree letting the sun bake her. She climbed down carefully clutching the fruit in the front of her dress. She stood on the river bank and called to the children in her native tongue, a low melodic call that reached them in the deepest areas where they dived and played. They came to her instantly, wet and shiny, hair bleached to variations of red and blond from the sun. They got out and then raced away from her, back to the sea shore, as fast on land as they were in the water.

She laughed as they flew with the exuberance of young, free, wild things. They entranced her, these beautiful children she had birthed. They kept her here, because how could she bear to leave them behind?

It was midday the next day and the fisherman was exhausted as the boat puttered to shore. The old man divided up the catch and gave him his smaller share. It wasn't a bad take really, there might even be a bit of money left over to buy one of the kids some new shoes for school. His spirits lifted as he approached the shack. Wary of her mood, he dropped the fish in the barrow and talked to her about his day. He hurriedly selected the children's fish from out of the batch and left her, eager to get on the main road and sell to the motorists who would be expecting him.

He was also anxious to be back by evening when her longing grew to its strongest. He had been very lucky until this last year, when her depression worsened. She was still able to keep her promise, but lately, at that hour, her sense of duty eroded.

It was a good day for the fisherman. He sold all the fish in record time and even got extra because two of his customers had large bills, and were too impatient to wait for change. His muscles rippled in his wiry arms and shoulders as he hoisted the barrow handles and pushed it home. The soles of his feet were tough as cow hide and he jogged across the asphalt to the sand with ease. He passed the madman, the Prophet, wrapped in robes walking in the other direction. The Prophet's ageless eyes pierced the fisherman and saw his secret.

When he got back to the hut, the children leaped around him and cheered when they saw the money, then they raced back to the sea. It was almost a shame summer was coming to an end. They turned gray with misery when they were cooped up in school all day.

He swept aside the net that served as a door to the hut, and greeted her, before turning the barrow upside down outside so the fish water and blood ran into the sand. He waved the notes at her and was gratified that she favored him with a smile. He wished the smile would reach her eyes.

She had over cooked the fish; a sign her mind had been wandering again, but he was so hungry he swallowed the dry flesh ravenously. The children bounded in with their usual energy and waited impatiently for their dinner. She served them with a growing air of detachment, her movements slow and deliberate.

She sat down with her own plate last and began her usual ritual of ripping the fish apart. He watched her for a few minutes trying to assess her mood, before he really looked at what she was doing. She took the heads off, set them aside and with her hard nails sliced into the fish. He stopped chewing.

She reached into the fish and took out the roe eating it first. She gave a small sound of pleasure and closed her eyes for a few blissful seconds. Suddenly she felt his stare. She opened her eyes and caught his look of dismay before he could disguise it. At the same moment she felt two distinct stirrings; one in her womb, and one from the sea.

They looked at each other for a long moment knowing exactly what the other was thinking. Even the children stopped eating as they became aware of the unnatural silence. They turned in unison looking first at him, and then at her.

How long had she been eating roe without realizing it? How foolish of her not to have guessed.

He wanted to break the silence, to tell her it was ok, that he was happy. He should say something.

"I'm going for a swim," she said and rose from the crate she had been sitting on. Her plate with the disemboweled fish clattered to the floor. He reached across and grabbed her wrist but her will was too strong. She dragged him after her without regard.

The sea leapt and rushed in anticipation. The stirring in her womb intensified and she knew this one was different from the others. This one was no hybrid; this one needed the sea.

He begged and commanded in turn as she strode to the water's edge. The children ran around them in agitated circles, wailing. Their sorrow tore at her heart but she knew that they would still thrive without her.

They all went into the surf together. She cried out loud from the joy; her salt tears mingled with sea spray. Her long-dry skin soaked in the healing minerals. Her body undulated and shook violently in the tumbling water.

He hugged her around the waist but nothing could stop her transformation. Her locks floated on the water around her, as the chemical reaction in her body created visible waves of energy. His tightly linked arms slipped down her waist as skin gave way to sleek scales, and legs melded into a single trunk.

He finally released her and she dove away from him into an oncoming wave. She fluked; her large blue-black tail slapped the wave and raised spray high into the air. The children swam with her in their first true union, darting around her like dolphins. Their bodies twisted and turned together; mother and offspring intertwined in a joyous race under the moonlight. They went with her as far out as they could and nuzzled her. Then they raced back to the shore; to him.

And she...dived to the depths carrying his last gift safely inside her womb, and returned to her people.

4. Down by the Riverside

It was already pitch black and he hadn't come yet. She was regretting her impulse to meet him here by the riverbank. She also wished she hadn't kept turning her flashlight on and off when she got bored. The batteries were low now, might not even light her all the way home. She stupsed to cover her nervousness.

No moon out tonight either, just a few fireflies teasing her with their tiny flashes of light. Boy, was she ever stupid. She glanced around quickly at the sound of grass swishing, but it was just some small animal moving through the bush.

Now c'mon girl, she chided herself, *you live your whole life in the country you know better than to get scared over every little noise.*

Still, she pulled her feet up under her even though the rock she was sitting on was uncomfortable. She tried to sit cross-legged but the jagged lines of the rock scraped her ankle-bones.

Memories of her granny's tales of spirits started to run through her mind. She hunched her shoulders and peered across the river.

She couldn't even tell what time it was, because the tiny wristwatch glowed dimly. After 6:00 p.m. she surmised from the deepening dark. She tried to get angry to hide her disappointment. What did she expect anyway? He'd probably found somebody more enticing than her to be with; the other village girls were certainly just as eager as she was.

She did think she was the best looking girl in Hope River, however. She had nice light brown skin, a full figure, and everybody praised her curly, long "good" hair.
She twirled a length of it around her finger. Tonight she had worn it loose hoping to trap him in it.

Pride kept her sitting on that rock on the river bank in the dark. She felt her breath quicken as anger began to swell in her.

Who he think he is anyway?

Didn't he realize how many guys would kill for a chance just to talk to her? She didn't let just any man step up to her. She had earned a reputation for being stuck up and conceited and that was just fine with her. She wasn't always going to be trapped in a small village; one day her mother was going to send for her to come live in New York, and then…yes then, they would all see she was somebody special. She snatched up her flashlight and slid down the rock heedless of the scratches on the back of her legs. She turned to go down the track, shaking the flashlight in hopes of jump-starting the batteries.

"Hey Lita," a male voice spoke from right behind her. She gave a startled exclamation and took a few quick steps forward before she caught herself. She shone the flashlight in his face and as the light came on suddenly, he grimaced, then grinned. Her emotions warred against each other, irritation and excitement battled before the excitement won. He took out a handkerchief and patted his lean, handsome face. She watched in fascination. He looked more Indian than black with his high cheekbones, dusky brown smooth skin, and thick curly hair. He had told her his mother was an East Indian and his father a Portuguese. His Guyanese accent sounded weird but nice. Even his scent was exotic, spicy.

He never took his eyes off her as he completed his mopping, and returned the hanky to his pocket.

"Sorry I'm late, I got a little lost," he laughed. She couldn't help smiling back.

"Well that's ok. I forgot we were meeting anyways. I always come to the river for a stroll at night," she lied. He nodded as though he believed her.

"Yes, I can guess how the river must be nice to watch on a dark night with no moon," he teased. She aimed the light near her face so he could see her toss her beautiful head.

They walked and chatted. He was casual as he spoke about college, visiting England, going to Costa Rica for something called spring break.

She tried to keep pace, teasing him so he wouldn't notice how little they had in common. They came to an area where the trees gave way to a little sandy area by the water's edge. He put his arm around her waist and stopped her. He took a deep breath of the crisp, night air and looked up at the stars. She hoped he couldn't hear how fast her heart was thumping.

He was going to kiss her; she just knew it, and then what? He was the most attractive boy she had ever met, but she didn't want to end up discarded. In her secret mind she was already picturing herself returning with him to England; a little premature but possible. He pulled her closer to him until their bodies touched, and she could feel rather than see him looking down at her. She closed her eyes in anticipation and waited.

He didn't kiss her.

She sensed his distraction and opened her eyes. He was looking across the river and not paying attention to her at all. She peered into the darkness and heard for the first time, the squeaking of soapy clothes being washed.

"What's that noise?" he asked but she couldn't respond because she was frozen, speechless with fear. Her grandmother's tales came flooding back.

She crouched down and he did the same. Across the tumbling water, a bent figure was leisurely hitting clothes against the rocks and humming in a sort of eerie off key way.

The person was washing clothes in the river at night. It was a strange thing that no normal villager would do.

It knew they were there. Lita was certain. Her heart was thumping again but not in excitement.

Oh Lawd!

What was going to happen to them? She shushed him when he tried to speak, mentally running through psalms, Hail Mary's, any protective mantras.

Suddenly, inspiration struck her.

She hurriedly un-buttoned her blouse and pulled her skirt off roughly. He was surprised but not to be outdone began to undo his belt. She turned her blouse on the wrong side and flipped her skirt inside out. He stopped fiddling with his belt buckle as he saw her put her clothes back on, seams out, labels showing.

"What is this?" he asked out loud in a suspicious tone.

She slapped her hand over his mouth, although she knew it was too late.

The thing that was washing clothes in the river stopped humming abruptly. She couldn't see it but she knew it was looking at them. Only the sound of the water could be heard, and the lack of any other noise became an ominous presence.

Suddenly, the sound of cloth hitting rocks came to them again; a few feet away-- on their side of the bank.

Lita gave a quick gasp and began scurrying back the path they had come. He followed her protesting.

They made it back to the main road to Lita's relief. Whatever moment they might have shared was lost forever and he was as eager to be away from her as she was to go home.

She refused to answer his questions. How could he possibly understand without her looking like a superstitious, ignorant, country girl? She couldn't bear that. It was better he leave thinking she was a tease.

At least she had saved his life tonight even if he didn't know it.

5. Amen

"God is good!" Pastor Clyde shouted.

"All the time!" the people shouted back. The band struck up another impossibly loud praise song, and soon everybody was shouting and waving to the calypso rhythm.

Rolle liked this part of church. He clapped his hands and sang, and admired Thomas's skill on the drums. Thomas was so good he could probably play for a carnival band. Rolle felt convicted for this thought and said a quick sorry to Jesus. Of course, Thomas was right where he belonged, using his talents for the Lord.

Pastor Clyde signaled to the praise team to change the tempo, as he moved into the reflective part of the service. The mood of the service changed to reverence. Hands raised to the air in supplication, bodies swayed slowly from left to right.

"All eyes closed, all hearts open, ask the Holy Spirit to come now and touch you," Pastor Clyde said softly into his microphone.

This was the part of church Rolle did not like. He swayed with the other kids from his Sunday school class, and closed his eyes. He prayed and then waited, but as usual nothing happened. He opened his eyes as an older woman began to speak in tongues.

"Yes sister, speak to us," Pastor Clyde said with eyes screwed tightly shut and head shaking slowly from side to side. The woman went on for some time until Rolle began to think she was having a different kind of visitation: the not-good kind; however, soon after that she stopped, and then one of the deacons' wives began the interpretation.

"Praise God for He is merciful," she began.

"Yes!" the people declared as one. The interpretation was much shorter to Rolle's relief.

He sat between his two closest friends from Sunday school class, Andre and Agnes. Agnes looked very pretty today, dressed in a velvet green dress some relative had sent her from overseas. Maybe they didn't know how hot it was under a tent. Her face was shiny already, and there were still hours to go.

He wasn't faring much better himself. He was sweating under the freshly ironed, and starched cotton collar of his long sleeve dress shirt.

Sometimes he wished church only went for an hour like the "Other" church his school friends went to. They went in, said some prayers, had communion, crossed themselves, and then went home.

Something was happening behind him at the back of the tent. He turned like everyone else and his jaw dropped. His mother, who was never late, was just arriving holding hands with the Prophet. The crazy, street character who screamed at everybody and constantly misquoted scriptures. The Prophet, who walked for miles barefoot, slept on the street, and probably ate out of the garbage.

Agnes and Andre were wide eyed, and Rolle wished he was anywhere but there. His mother marched the Prophet up to the altar. The Prophet looked like how Rolle felt. Actually he looked worse. His wild eyes darted over the congregation and his mouth moved wordlessly. His whole posture was of someone seeking to flee at the first opportunity.

"Brothers and sisters," Rolle's mother said a little breathlessly, "All of you know that this man is the one we call the Prophet."

"Yes, yes," the people answered.

"Well, you know and I know he is not a real prophet. He is a false prophet," she said in a matter-of-fact tone.

"True, true," the people murmured. The Prophet flinched and tried to haunch his tall, sparse frame into a smaller ball of humanity. Rolle wished his mother would stop embarrassing him, the man, and herself, but it was about to get worse; oh, so much worse.

She took a deep breath and announced, "This man's real name is Robert Johnson Windsor, and he is my distant cousin."

Agnes gasped and then she, Andre, and the other kids burst out into stifled titters. Rolle stared at the dirt floor, and wondered if it would be kind enough to swallow him whole.

The Prophet stayed for the service. He let the church's senior staff lay hands on him and pray for his deliverance. Then he sat quietly while Pastor Clyde gave his sermon. At first.

"Moses knew they must slay the lamb to take away the sins of the people, for the adultery and fornication and riotous living!" Pastor Clyde shouted.

"You are one good preacher!" The Prophet shouted back.

Rolle covered his face with one hand and sank deeper into his chair. People chuckled and Pastor Clyde gave an indulgent smile.

"Christ is the lamb of God. We don't have to fear death! Christ has come to take away the sins of the world!" Pastor Clyde continued.

"Yes everything you say is true!" the Prophet called out with equal vigor.

This went on for another ten minutes with Pastor Clyde slowly losing control of his service. He gripped the podium and hollered all the louder. The Prophet's running commentary echoed back even stronger. People walking on the road next to the tent stopped to see what the extra yelling was about. Rolle's Mother was obviously distressed, and she tried to shush the Prophet, but he had lost his shyness and was back to being a loud mouth, crazy man. He really seemed to be enjoying himself.

Pastor Clyde gave up and closed the service almost forty minutes earlier than usual. Rolle's mother was mortified but decided that this was just one of the burdens of saving a lost soul. The Prophet stood as the last hymn began, and smiled tenderly at Rolle's mother, revealing surprisingly good teeth.

"Nice to see you, Lucille. You grow up real nice and everything," he said.

"Robert, stay with us. You don't need to live on the road, you have family," she urged.

Rolle held his breath in horror.

"Is ok, God watch over me anywhere I pass," The Prophet replied, gathering his robes with a dignity Rolle had to admire.

The old man turned to leave, walking towards the back of the tent with his head held high. Just as he was about to go through the flaps, he called out to Pastor Clyde who was still trying to recover, "Thank you Pastor, for a wonderful service! I like this church. It is a nice church."

Pastor Clyde gave a faltering smile, but it fell away as the Prophet swept through the flaps with a parting shot, "See you next Sunday!"

6. The Neighbours

"Where am I going again?" Sonny murmured to himself as he patted his front, then back pants pockets in turn. His mother looked at him over her glasses and frowned.

"What are you talking about?" She asked, "It's 7:30 in the morning. Where else would you be going to, except work?"

He looked at her sitting in her favourite paisley upholstered rocking chair.

His forehead creased in puzzlement, "I am?"

"Sonny what is the matter with you? This is the fourth or fifth time this week you can't remember where you going," she dropped the *St.Marts Chronicle* onto her lap.

She must really be worried to give up her crossword, he thought.
He stared back at her for a few minutes, genuinely confused. As she normally did whenever worried, she stuck out her lower lip.

"Ok, I'm going to work. But where are my keys then?" he asked, and resumed patting his pockets.

"Check your pants from yesterday, or on top the fridge," she said. Her faded brown eyes narrowed.

"I checked there already," he said, beginning to get frustrated.

"Sonny…did you take anything from Ms. Lester?" Suspicion sharpened her voice to a screech.
He jumped and his gaze shifted away from hers. She clenched the *Chronicle* in her gnarled fists.

"Sonny, answer me!"

"Ok, take it easy," he said trying to sound more assertive. "Yes, she brought a soup last week, and I was hungry so I had some," he admitted, hoping to placate her.

His mother threw the newspaper to the ground.

"Stupid! I warned you about her! Her hands are "dirty!" She and that child are not right and you took food from her?"

His initial confusion now cleared, Sonny squared his massive shoulders and said, "Ma, I'm a grown man of 28. If I want to eat some soup, I can and I will. I don't know where you get this stupidness about witchcraft from."

"Oh yeah? Then how comes almost every morning for this week you wake up and don't know where you are half the time? You don't know where you're going or you can't find your keys? You're going to lose your job!" his mother retorted. She eased herself painfully out of the chair and her knees creaked. She winced and hobbled off to the kitchen, grumbling under her breath about children who thought they were so grown they could be rude to their parents. Well, in her day, such a thing was unheard of!

Sonny wiped his face with his large hand wearily. He dwarfed the living room with his tall, muscular frame, looking out of place amidst the plethora of crochet and ceramics. He stood for a few moments contemplating the Lesters.

Women told him constantly that he was attractive and fit. He liked to think he wasn't vain about it all but, yes, women threw themselves at him and he let them. Sometimes even mothers made overtures on behalf of their daughters, which both fascinated and creeped him out. But he'd never experienced anything like the Lesters before.

He turned gingerly in the room as he searched for his keys, trying not to upset the little display tables nor knock over his mother's genuine imitation Royal Doulton collection.
Why did his mother have to think up such craziness? He wondered. Dirty hands…such rubbish.

"I found them!" he announced with relief as he spied his key ring on the window sill of the living room window. He grabbed it up and glanced out between the lace curtains.

Ms. Lester looked straight back at him from her bay window in the house across the street. She smiled as she saw him and waved enthusiastically. He nodded quickly in acknowledgement, and headed for the front door.

"Sonny, I warn you: don't have anything to do with that woman or her daughter! People say they see them in the cemetery at night doing all kinds of evil things!" His mother cautioned as she stood at the kitchen door. He was dismayed at the tremor in her voice, and the gleam of tears in her eyes. He shook off the guilt.

"People need to find hard work to do and stop gossiping," he snapped. He left the house, slamming the door behind him.

He was a little startled but not completely surprised to see Lucia Lester standing by the driver's cab of his delivery truck. He supposed her mother had sent her out to meet him. Lucia was a cute girl, but way too young. She was 15 or 16 he surmised. Right now she was giving him a very mature and challenging look. She was also wearing black shorts that exposed her well-shaped legs, and a pink polka dot tank top or tube top, he wasn't sure which. He tried not to stare at the visible portion of her ample cleavage.

"You going to work, Sonny?" she asked, smiling.

She tossed her long braids and he had to smirk. Who did she think she was fooling with all that fake hair?

"Yep," he said. She was leaning against the driver's side. He would have to brush or push past her to open it. He stood and waited.
I'm not going to jail for you, he thought.

"You should stay home one day. Hang out with me instead," she invited. She licked her full top lip slowly, wiping off some of the thick lipstick.

Sonny glanced at his watch and swore, "I'm late. Move please!"

She got off the door with exaggerated slowness, keeping his gaze. She brushed past him, letting her breast graze his arm. Her scent was unlike anything he'd ever smelt before. It was earthy, rich with spice. He couldn't help inhaling. He got into the truck and swore again, trying to ignore his body's response.

"Jail!" he muttered out loud. He started up the truck and drove to the first stop on his list.

As he tried to avoid the worst of the pot holes on the feeder road leading up to EverGreen Labs, the truck shook violently. The undercarriage scraped loudly against a boulder that he couldn't avoid and he winced. Really – you'd think government or the Americans with all their money would pay for a decent road.

He forgot about how bad the road was once he got up to the Lab. He got out the truck and sighed at the full coat of red mud splashed along its sides. He grabbed his ID tag out of his pockets and approached the main gate cautiously. It gave him the creeps coming here. It was always so eerily silent. Even the birds refused to sing in the trees that surrounded the large white, bunker-style building. He went through the usual process of showing his ID and submitting to a pat-down.

The legend that locals weren't allowed in the Lab wasn't strictly true. The armed security guards were local, albeit it strangely aggressive. Through the small windows of the double doors leading from the reception area, he'd glimpsed other people there too. The only one he'd ever recognized was the Prophet. He assumed the people he'd seen were local because they weren't wearing lab coats. He himself had never seen the heart of the Lab where all the weird experiments were rumoured to take place.

The ebony goddess who was the office receptionist, was also local.

"Hey Shirley," he flashed her a brilliant smile.

This girl was a tough nut but he liked that. She'd turned him down for a drink countless times - some nonsense about his Casanova reputation.

She pursed her luscious lips while she glanced at her schedule, and what she said next wiped the smile off his face.

"Noo… you're not supposed to be here today," she arched a perfect penciled eyebrow.

Sonny rubbed his chin. He was known for his excellent memory. So much so, he could hear his schedule once and remember it without fault. It was his thing. His boss had even stopped giving him paper copies of his delivery stops.

But that had changed over the last week. It had been terrible. He hadn't told his mother about his memory lapses. He definitely didn't want to tell her that every day for the last five days or so he had found himself at Ms. Lester's front gate.

Sometimes, it had been in the mornings, once in the afternoon, most times late at night. Each time he had come to himself just as he was about to go through their little gate, or knock on their door. He would stumble away confused and disoriented. Even now, as he was here with Shirley, Lucia's distinct perfume lingered in his nostrils.
The memory of a hot bowl of pig tail broth came to his mind now.
Nonsense! He said to himself sternly.
He mumbled an excuse to Shirley, who warned him she would have to tell his boss about the unscheduled stop.

By lunch, when each delivery stop confirmed he was in the wrong place at the wrong time, he had had enough. He called in sick, and spent the afternoon driving along the coastal road to cool his fevered brain. Driving always relaxed him and it was the perfect remedy. He was even amused, when he drove past a man in an expensive looking suit, struggling to put a goat in the back of an SUV.

He felt the tension ease out of him as the wind rushed by his face, and the sunlit highway lay open before him. Evening rolled around, and he drove back into town and stopped at Scorpio's rum shop. He played a few rounds of dominos, had a couple of stiff drinks, and cheered up.

He got home late, and tried to turn the key in the lock quietly to avoid waking his mother. The last thing he wanted was another argument.
She was in her rocking chair, waiting for him. He sighed as he closed the door.

Ah boy…

"Sonny, sit down. We need to talk."

He reluctantly sat on the sofa adjacent to her chair. Her voice was surprisingly soft so he began to feel hopeful of avoiding a tirade. They sat silently in the stuffy room. The heat of the alcohol combined with the humid night began to give him a headache. The sweat on the back of his neck began to soak into the velour fabric of the sofa. He began to feel itchy and longed for a cold shower. Still, he sat and waited. His mother's gaze held steady on their closed front door.

"Before your father got…sick, he was having an affair with Ms. Lester," she said.

He chewed at the inside of his bottom lip wondering if he should tell her he'd known that for years; common gossip. His father wasn't the only man in the neighbourhood to visit the Lester house.

"She and the child had just moved in across the street. They came from a village deep in the interior." She paused and cleared her throat.

"I know, Mum," he said, hoping to spare her the painful recounting, but she ignored him.

"They say the women from up there are nasty. They bewitch men," she nodded her head as though in agreement with herself. Sonny grunted. There were quite a few secluded villages in the rainforest interior which one would have to hike to get into. Landslides and road disrepair had all but cut off a few. He had heard of the curiously inbred, isolated village where the Lesters were from.

He yawned widely and scratched at the wet, short curls at the back of his neck. The polyester fibers of the sofa stuck to his skin driving him crazy with the itching. Idly, he reflected that he didn't blame Ms. Lester for his father. His father was a grown man who made his own choices.

"Your father," she said as though she'd read his thoughts, "He was a good man, really nice, very kind to everybody. She used that against him." Her voice shook. He got up and stooped next to her chair.

"I'll never leave you," he covered her clenched fists with his hand and squeezed.

She looked at him teary eyed and replied, "That's not what I mean. You need your own family."

Sonny wasn't prone to deep self-reflection. He didn't bother to question why he had no inclination to marry, father a child and all that. Their family's story wasn't so strange; a middle-aged math teacher had an affair with an attractive younger neighbor, and cleaned out his family's savings to court her. He died of some unknown wasting disease a year later. Good thing too, as he had been about to sign over their house to Ms. Lester. Sonny did not know who had seduced who, but he didn't hold a grudge against the lady. It was all distant history.

He helped his mother out of the chair and up the stairs, being patient because of her arthritis. She begged him yet again to be careful.

Even upstairs there was no relief from the humid night, and he tossed restlessly. He got up, wiped his chest, back and underarms with a towel, and opened his bedroom window to gulp in the sparse breeze. The neighborhood was in darkness except for the lone street light. Beyond, he could see up Mount Fran, where lights from the wealthier homes glittered at various elevations. The Lester house in front of him was still and dark. He lay down again on his back and drifted off eventually.

A reddish glow filtered through his eyelids, and he frowned, disturbed. He opened them and blearily tried to focus. The glow was coming from the ceiling. As his vision cleared, he realized there were actually two pin point red lights, and they were coming from something else that was on the ceiling. He stared, and it moved.

A large spider, he realized. The glowing red lights were its eyes. He had never seen that before. The room was filled with a familiar aroma. Uneasy, he decided to get up and knock it off the ceiling, and discovered something strange.

He couldn't move.
He struggled to raise his right hand until sweat broke out on his forehead. His breath came fast and he tried to force himself upright.

He couldn't move.

Ma! He tried to call out, but nothing came out. He couldn't even whisper. He tried closing his eyes and found he could no longer blink. He was paralyzed. His heart hammered as he helplessly stared up at the spider. The red glow from its eyes seemed to spread until a haze filled the room. The familiar odour intensified; a mélange of spices.

He now became aware of a growing weight on his chest that was stealing his breath away. He gasped as the weight grew and then it stopped, pinning him to the bed. The red haze cleared, and he found he could move his eyeballs enough to see the thing on his chest that was slowly suffocating him.

Lucia.
At least, it resembled Lucia. He could make out her features, but she looked…raw. Her skin was oily and shiny, and her eyes were completely red. Even in the dark, he could see she had no pupils or irises. She smiled and he felt faint.

"I want you," she whispered.

 She traced the hair around his nipples and he felt his body respond.

"Mama say I'm too young to take you by myself," she giggled and he felt droplets of sweat roll off his forehead down into his ears. She reached out a finger that was tipped with a pointed claw and touched his bare eyeball. His chest heaved.

"Delicious," her voice was a hiss.

She easily lifted his brawny right arm and sunk her fangs into it.
He stared, horrified as his flesh gave way. Her scent enveloped him. She eased off his chest and he noticed her own bosom was heaving. The odour began to clear. His fingers twitched…

"Sonny, get up! You late for work!"

His mother's voice penetrated his stupor. He opened his eyes and was shocked to see sunlight, full and bright, flooding his bedroom. He blinked. His eyes were dry and irritated. He slowly sat up.

What…?

His mother knocked on the door and called again.

"Sonny!"

"Ok, ok!" he answered, his voice cracking. He swallowed past a dry throat. He sat up slowly, his body aching. He glanced down at his forearms and froze.

On his left arm, halfway between his wrist and the crook of his arm, were two small puncture marks. He felt his pulse quicken.

No.

He still didn't quite believe what he had seen, but one thing was clear, somehow Lucia had gotten into his room and had bitten him. He grabbed a pair of jeans, put them on quickly, and opened the door. He ran past his startled mother, who called after him,

"Boy, you're not wearing a shirt!"

Rage enveloped him as he stalked across to the Lester's house and wrenched open the little, white wrought iron gate. He ran up to the door and pounded on it until its glass inlay shook.

Ms. Lester opened the door and peered out, her face frightened at first, but then her expression turned to surprise. He stood for a moment, his nostrils flared.

Her voice quavered, "Sonny?"

She looked so perturbed, standing there in her blue floral nightie and fluffy bedroom slippers. He took in the hair net wrapped around her gray bun, and the spatula she was holding. Behind her, sitting at a table in the kitchen, Lucia was poised with a fork in front of a plate of johnny cakes. The smell of cocoa, and frying saltfish wafted through the air. They both stared at him, perplexed.

I must be crazy.

Sonny glanced down at the marks on his arm. A spider had bitten him during the night and he had a nightmare. That was all.

"Sorry, Ms. Lester, I..." he scratched his head and tried to think of an excuse. It was so embarrassing.

"That's ok, son, come in and have some breakfast. I insist." She smiled and he was aware that she was still an attractive woman.

There was indeed a large plate of johnny cakes on the table, way more than two women could possibly eat. They were golden brown and smelled delicious. His mouth watered.

"I made them for you," Ms. Lester said and stepped back so he could come in.

How did she know he was coming? He suddenly detected the spicy odour underneath the smell of fried food. It was compelling. Lucia gave him a mischievous wink and blew him a kiss.

His feet were urging him forward but he was reluctant to go in. Something was off. If anybody had behaved the way he just had, at his mother's door, he would be punching heads, not inviting the miscreant in for breakfast.

His right foot stepped over the threshold.

What...how did that happen? His eyes bulged.

"Kids don't listen," Ms. Lester said, and glanced back at Lucia frowning in mock anger.

He didn't want to go in but he couldn't stop himself. The scent was twice as strong as it had been in his room. His thinking muddled.

"I told her time and time again, you need patience to catch a man," she shook her head ruefully.

He opened his mouth to protest and found he couldn't utter a sound.
He was suddenly scared; more scared than the night before.
He put both his hands on either side of the door frame to stop himself going in.

"We're just two poor women, dependent on your kindness," her eyes widened and he saw she had no pupils. Lucia stood up, and what she was wearing was far from decent.

Sweat broke out under his armpits and forehead. A force was actually pulling him into the house. It took all his strength not to go in.

"You'll need a job with more money, and I think it's time you give me your house," Ms. Lester said.

He knew; he just knew if he stepped over the threshold he would never leave again. Ms. Lester took another step backwards into the kitchen, her smile broadened.

"I hope you have more stamina than your daddy, Sonny!" she laughed.

Sunshine beat down on his bare back. How could this happen in broad daylight?

The sound of something scattering on the floor distracted all of them. He glanced down with difficulty and saw grains of white rice spinning in all directions.

Ms. Lester and Lucia snapped their heads back and forth trying to follow the movement of the grains. Sonny felt the force ease on his forward momentum and he gasped and stepped back. His mother grabbed his right bicep with considerable force for an old woman and dragged him away from the doorway. He stumbled after her, looking over his shoulder, fascinated by the sight of Ms. Lester and her daughter on their hands and knees chasing down the rice on their kitchen floor.

His mother, dropped another handful of rice in front of the Lester's front gate, her face set hard. They hurried across the street. He opened their front door and let her in first. He closed the door quickly and bolted it, shaking. He turned slowly, resting his back on the door and staring at her with wide eyes.

She put on her bifocals and picked up the day's Chronicle from her arm chair, and then she swatted him across the head with the rolled up paper.

"Didn't I tell you to stay away from that woman?"

She sat in her arm chair painfully, unrolled the paper and began to read.

"It's time they went back to the bush," she said without taking her eyes off her reading.

And so he waited until the sun had just slipped out of view below the horizon. He set the blaze at the back of the Lester's wooden home, making sure to use lots of kerosene oil, and then went around to the front to pound on the door for the second time that day.

 They came out, two frightened, crying women as they watched their home burn.

The women of the street watched from their verandahs, and behind curtains, while their husbands and sons battled the blaze with heedless abandon. But by the time the fire truck arrived, it was much too late.

Since no wife in the neighbourhood would give them shelter, the Lesters moved on.

7. The Post Office

Town Council member Peter Woods was handing out flyers in front of the post office for the second time that week. The people who accepted the flyers knew it was no use. The post office staff knew it was no use. Peter Woods himself knew it was no use. He was handing out flyers in Lloyd Johnson's town, and Lloyd had been mayor for eleven years straight, and would probably die in office. But Peter was stubborn and insisted on going through with his campaign activities, so he gave hearty laughs and slapped people on their backs, as he thrust flyers into their unwilling hands.

Rolle stomped up the steps to the front doors of the post office in a foul mood. He was oblivious to the beautiful landscaping around the quaint, colonial style building and to the purity of the azure sky above. He marched past the potted plants and croton hedges that lined the verandah and almost bowled Peter Woods over. Woods put out a steadying hand on the taller man's chest.

"Hey, Pardna, take it easy!" Woods exclaimed with a broad smile. Rolle responded by pushing Woods square in the chest and making him overbalance. The portly man slipped on some of the discarded flyers at his feet and landed solidly on his bottom. He yelped and swore as loud laughter came from customers in line. Rolle stalked into the building without a backward glance, and went to his desk behind the counter. His friend and co-worker Agnes raised her eyebrows as he slammed drawers and raised dust.

"Rolle, you need to cool down," she said. He glared at her and plopped down in his chair. He stared blindly at the mahogany wood desk in front of him, trying to lose his rage in the wood's whorls and rings. Agnes glanced around and her face fell as she noticed their supervisor was watching Rolle. She pushed some paper around her own desk and spoke quietly.

"White has you under observation, boy. Take it easy, ok, you don't need the trouble."

Rolle made a derisive noise and slowly wiped his face with his hand, pulling his long features into a basset hound expression; however, Agnes was right. He had enough problems. Problems upon problems.

There was a middle-age German tourist waiting for his section to open. She stared at him with a wary expression as he slowly took out his small "Open" sign and put it on his desk.

The tourist, who said her name was Gina, went on and on about philately. He kept a pleasant, blank face as she raved about the *Warblers of the Caribbean* series. He didn't have the first clue about her beloved hobby, having just been transferred two days ago. Nobody wanted to deal with the avid stamp collectors. They were all a little weird. The postal workers laughed about it all the time; imagine collecting stamps as a hobby. Talk about needing to get a life.

Rolle's anger dissipated into something more manageable so he was able to give Gina the stamps she wanted, overcharging her by ten dollars out of habit. He smoothly pocketed the extra cash and put the rest of the money in the till. The hours till closing at 4:00 p.m. loomed, giving him too much time to think about Lita.

He turned down lunch with Agnes who went down to the cafeteria looking peeved.

Man, you take a girl out once and she makes a big deal out of it. It's not like she didn't know I had a girlfriend…'had' being the operative word, he thought.

He watched as the other cashiers continued to serve customers during the lunch hour while he remained with his chin propped up in one hand. He didn't mind not working. In fact, that's why he hadn't fought the transfer. Such a grand term: "transfer", when all he had done was to move across the room. The cool breeze coming through the window on his right was helpful and the view wasn't too bad either. He forgot his woes for a moment as he watched the bank tellers coming back from lunch.

St.Marts really has some pretty girls, he mused.

His improved mood disappeared, as he suddenly saw his ex-best friend Andre running up the street towards the post office. He must be mad to come and tackle Rolle at work.

Rolle was on his feet and already out the front door when Andre arrived sweating, and breathing heavily. Andre's left cheek was swollen and discolored from their brief meeting earlier that morning.

Andre started gesturing while Rolle crossed his arms and glared at him.

"Man, Rolle why you didn't give me a chance to explain, man? You think you do right? You just come out swinging and don't even give me a chance to explain? I can't believe we friends for so long and you turn on me like that," Andre complained.

Rolle thought about giving him a souvenir on his right cheek to match the left.

He looked down on the shorter man with disdain, "So explain."

He flexed the bruised knuckles on his right hand. The movement was not lost on Andre. Andre put a hand to his waist and rubbed the sweat off his brow as he seemed to think of what he could say. The early morning incident seemed like a bad dream in the heat of midday. Both men could not resist the memory.

Rolle unwillingly recalled his call to Lita; his suspicions roused by a rumor going around the post office. Agnes had broken it to him as kindly as she could, but nothing could dull the pain that lanced through him once he heard it.

So he called Lita when he was supposed to have been on his way to work. She took long to answer, her voice heavy and deep with sleep. He told her he was on his way over to her house. Her voice grew sharp and she asked him what was going on, but he hung up. Since he was already parked outside her house all he had to do was wait. Almost immediately, Andre came out her front door looking disheveled and tense. Rolle could not believe it. He did not remember getting out of his car, the blood pounding in his head.

He vaguely recalled Lita screaming at him and Andre trying to run away. What words were spoken? Had he said anything? How had he driven to work through the red haze of rage?

Andre was still struggling for words, which was quite a predicament for a lawyer.

"Rolle man, have I ever done anything like this before? I thought we were tight, how you just jump to conclusions without checking all the facts first?"

Rolle's contempt was almost tangible.

"You can't even be a man and tell me the truth? I catch you red-handed and you such a liar you can't tell me the truth?" The muscles in his neck popped as he took a step forward.

Andre's mouth opened and closed, and he stared at the irate Rolle for a few minutes. Out of the corner of his eye, Rolle saw several curious faces looking at them through the post office windows.

Everybody knew what this was about. Andre swore under his breath and squared his shoulders. He made an elaborate show of tying his power red and blue tie, and tucking his shirt into his trousers. He put on his best contract negotiation game-face and lowered his tone.

"Alright man, truth? You want truth? You'll get it then. Lita found out about all those little women you have on the side, all of them! Even the one you have in New York. She got real upset, crying and behaving crazy. She call me over because she wanted me to tell her it wasn't true, I didn't mean for anything to happen between us but it did, so deal with it!"

With that he spun on his heel and stalked back up the road to where his Mazda was parked. Rolle watched him go, his mouth agape. Andre got into the car and peeled off. And just like that, 20 years of friendship ended.

Rolle went back to his desk, deeply disturbed, but also puzzling over how Lita could have found out about New York Sarah. Only a few people knew the truth behind his Labour Day holidays in the U.S. Of course it could have been Andre himself who had told Lita.

Four o'clock took forever to come. He was about to turn his little "Open" sign to its "Closed" side when Postmaster General White walked over and dropped a large manila envelope on his desk.

"These are some new sheets just issued. Update the inventory then put them on display. Try to make sure you market them when the customers come by, the ministry is trying these out as a sample."

He fixed Rolle with a stern stare.

"Please do not toss these into a drawer and forget about them as you are prone to do. The ministry specifically wants to know if these do well with the tourists."

Rolle grunted, and roughly tore open the envelope. White let out an irritated exclamation,

"Be careful!"

Rolle lounged back in his chair and flipped through sheets with insolent indifference. More birds and flora; $35U.S. a sheet. They were nice he had to admit. The colors were vibrant and tropical. They almost had a 3-D appearance; the lines were not quite sharply defined. He put them back in the envelope and with a bit of dramatic flair, opened his top draw and let the envelope fall in. Rolle turned his sign and stood up, dwarfing the older man by over a foot. Rolle picked up his satchel and loped off.

Agnes was waiting for him outside looking hopeful.

"You want to go get a drink?" she indicated with her head to the bar further down the boulevard.

He was about to refuse but thought, what else was there to do? Usually he would go over to Lita's. He shrugged his assent and strolled with her to the Scorpio Bar, oblivious as before to the beauty around him. Agnes tried to get him to look at the yachts anchored off the marina because she knew he liked boats. He nodded as she pointed out the catamaran that was anchored some distance off shore. There was a red-haired woman catching the rays of the setting sun on the boat. She was wearing a very striking, florescent green bikini. Rolle ogled for a few moments but his heart wasn't in it.

Inside Scorpio's, he let Agnes order the drinks, and tried to focus on other things. But how could he when there were couples all around him? There were tourist women with tour guides, young professionals and executives showing off their trophy girlfriends, and teenagers acting brash and loud.

Agnes tried to advise him on matters of the heart. He would get over it, she promised. He knew she was right. He was good looking, slim, muscled and tall. Even now he could see a group of women checking him out and giggling.

"I loved that girl," he told Agnes quietly.

Agnes sighed, pursing her full lips into a pout. There were two executive types looking her over from their bar stools. Rolle scrutinized her. He had been cured of his brief interest in her after their first date. She was too…available. Now with his ego wounded, and those guys looking at him enviously, he took a second look. She was a voluptuous girl, full breasted with cocoa brown skin. She dressed sexy: miniskirts and low cut blouses. She was attractive in a rather flamboyant way, but he couldn't help comparing her to Lita's natural beauty. Lita…with her long, curly hair and graceful limbs. Lita glided rather than walked. She was an elegant creature that he loved to admire. He looked at Agnes's mouth resplendent in its scarlet lipstick, and compared it with the classy, pink gloss Lita swore by.

He touched Agnes's cheek and she glanced up at him startled. She leaned into him and they kissed for a brief moment. He realized it was a mistake almost immediately. She tried to put her arms around his neck to the delight of the executive types watching them. He firmly held her wrists and put her hands on the table. To take the sting out of the rejection, he covered them with his own large hands.

"I shouldn't have done that Agnes, sorry."

She blinked and looked away, her hurt obvious in the rigid lines of her posture. He sighed wearily. What a messed up day. Agnes turned on him.

"You have all these girls Rolle, and none of them can do anything for you. You just playing around here and all over the world like you'll be young forever. When you going to settle down man? You're already 34!" Her voice rose sharply. He was beginning to remember why he didn't date co-workers.

"And as for Lita, Lita, Lita! I'm so sick of hearing about that little country girl like she some kind of angel or saint. Well, we all know better now, don't we?" She stood up but something she said triggered his interest.

He grabbed her wrist and pulled her slowly down towards him. Even in her anger he could see that she thought he might kiss her again. He looked her in the eye and said, "What was that about me playing all over the world?"

She realized her mistake, but being Agnes she was defiant, "Yes, Rolle. I know about the girl in New York, and I told Lita. She deserved to know what a rat you really are," she said.

Rolle could have cheerfully slapped her.

"You lie, Agnes. You wanted to break us up so you could get a chance with me. You're so pathetic and transparent." He let go of her wrist and left. He did not pay the bill.

He parked, as was his custom, on the front lawn of his parents' home. His father was not interested in lawn maintenance so there was no conflict about that at least. He went into the bungalow, slamming the green door behind him. His father was playing dominos on an old card table. He looked over his glasses at Rolle and went on with his solitary game. Rolle went through the living room into the kitchen, and hugged his mother as she stirred up rice and peas on the stove.

"Oh Rolle, I was wondering when you'd get home. Lita's been calling for you. She sounded worried." She lovingly patted his cheek.

I'll bet, Rolle thought dryly.

She dished out stewed snapper and rice and peas for him, while singing about telling Jesus all of her troubles. He had to smile. His mother was one woman who never had troubles; she was always smiling.

"I baked a cake. It's on the counter under the food cover cooling. Try to get a slice before your dad discovers it's there, ok?" She laughed and went back to humming. Soon she would go upstairs and get dressed for prayer meeting. Then she would come downstairs and ask him and his father to come with her. They would make up some excuse; she would nod and leave, still humming to herself.

Rolle, perhaps because he was in such a contemplative mood, looked closely at his mother when she went through this routine. He was surprised to see that behind her cheerful acceptance of his refusal, there was real sorrow in her eyes. He knew church and God were important to her, and to him too, he supposed on some level. Still he had never bothered to think about what his constant rejection was doing to her. After she left, he sat in the living room watching T.V. His father continued his game and the usual silence followed, then his father said, "You want a game Rolle?"

Rolle was suspicious but figured he already knew what was coming. He turned his arm chair around to face the card table while his father shuffled the tiles. Rolle's hand was mainly sixes; it was probably going to be a short game. He made a show of studying his tiles like he had a strategy. His father actually cracked a smile as Rolle slammed a tile down on the table.

"Take it easy, son. The game just start."

They played for a while and then the inevitable happened.

"So how's the job going?" his father asked.

Rolle sighed. "It's ok."

"So you give any thought to what we talk about last week?"

His father got up and headed to the kitchen. His father came back with two huge chunks of cake on a plate. Rolle studied the game. He was losing of course. His father took a bite of cake, and drank from a glass of lemonade.

"You're a bright boy, Rolle. You were always coming home with first place in primary school."

Rolle tuned him out. First place out of a class of fifty eight-year-olds; it was laughable. His parents could not forget those few shining moments in grade three.

"…if you'd only apply yourself, and stop messing around with all these girls." His father's aggrieved voice penetrated Rolle's cocoon.

"Dad, I have a government job and that's what you wanted, isn't it?"

Rolle played his last six.

"Selling stamps? That's a job?" his father retorted.

Rolle got up, went into his room and closed the door.

The next day, work started off on its usual high note. Rolle was called into White's office to explain why he had knocked a prominent politician to the ground. Rolle had completely forgotten about the incident with Peter Woods. Woods had not forgotten about him though, and was demanding a written apology.

White told Rolle to turn in the apology by the end of the day.

"If not I'm afraid we'll have to review your future at this establishment," White said looking smug. Rolle wanted to laugh. He found himself echoing his father.

"Selling stamps? You must be crazy. He blocked my way. He's lucky all I did is push him!"

Rolle stalked out of White's office before the other could respond. He sat down at his desk and began thinking about job applications, as customers started coming in.

The German lady, Gina, had come back because she'd received a letter from the Philately office. Rolle as usual was in the dark about these things, so he asked her if she had the letter with her. She handed it to him with slight hesitation, as though afraid there had been some mistake. He read it a few times before it dawned on him that she had been personally invited to receive a whole sheet of the new 35 dollar stamps, for free.

He gave them to her and watched her walk away to a nearby booth where she took out an envelope and began addressing it. Agnes, dressed to impress, walked back and forth in front of him. He obligingly ogled her short skirt but did not talk to her.

When he glanced back at Gina, she was doing something very strange. She was licking a stamp, over and over. He stared as the strange behavior continued. When she had licked one stamp she seemed to be reluctant to stick it to the letter. She put it on and to his amazement pulled it off and began licking it again more agitatedly. Stamp collectors-- weird.

Rolle looked away, feeling as though he was witnessing some intimate happening, and glanced out the window instead. The red-haired woman he had noticed on the yacht the day before was coming down the road. She was wearing a lime green sundress that set off her tan and red hair. She came into the post office and after speaking to one of the tellers came up to his desk.

He was surprised. He wouldn't have pegged her as a collector. As it turned out she wasn't.

"Hi! I got this note asking me to pick up some new stamps for my husband?"

She smiled. He turned on the charm and smiled back. She was one of those tourists who told locals their whole life story; her name was Inga and her husband was on assignment with EverGreen Labs on Mount Fran and she saw little of him due to his work. She was so bored and lonely. Maybe he knew of some local hot spots to visit? Rolle assured her a personal guided tour.

She looked at the free sheet of stamps with surprise.

"Well it doesn't look like the type my hubby's into, but I guess he's not going to turn down a freebie."

She shrugged again and examined the sheet. She stopped smiling abruptly. She swayed.

"Are you ok?" Rolle stood up and automatically put his hand under her elbow.

She seemed startled as though out of a daze, and gave him a nervous smile.

"I don't know…I just feel a little dizzy. I guess it's the heat."

She slowly tore off one of the stamps along the perforated edge and held it up to her nose. Rolle frowned slightly as she tasted the underside with the tip of her tongue. But then she gave a little laugh, put the sheet back into the envelope, and continued to flirt with him.

When she left, he sat at his desk brooding. Agnes walked past him again, her high heels clicking loudly on the wood floor. One of the other tellers called after her, "Girl, you gonna wear a groove in the floor at that rate." The others laughed. It was 9:00 a.m.

At about a quarter to ten, two more tourists showed up to get their free new sheets. Rolle was getting fed up. He wandered how many more interruptions he was going to have to endure before lunch. He also wanted to know why the new stamps were being given away as it afforded him no opportunity to make a little extra on the side as usual. He delayed going into White's office until his curiosity got the better of him.

"Ok, Mr. White, what's the deal with these new stamps? How comes we're giving them away?" Rolle demanded. White raised an eyebrow.

"If you'd read your rules and regulations when you took on this job Mr.Trelfor, you would know that when a new stamp is issued in this country, we offer free samples to members of the International Philately Society."

Rolle's eyebrows shot up. There was a Society?

"I suppose they pay dues?" he hazarded a guess.

"The Society's members are all foreign nationals and pay in various currencies, which for convenience is handled by the Post Master's secretary. But you already knew that I'm sure," White's sarcastic tone did not bother Rolle, as he was too busy feeling peeved.

"Why aren't the dues paid through me?" he demanded. *All those lovely Euro notes*!

White picked up the phone and looked out of his office where he had a clear view of Rolle's desk.

"Do you have that letter of apology written up and signed yet? And I see you have customers waiting." White spoke into the phone asking for an outside line.

Rolle went back to his desk and issued out another five sheets. The morning wore on. Lunch break was at 1:00 p.m. and he spent the hour chatting to the other tellers and joking around much to Agnes's annoyance.

At 2:00 p.m. he turned his "Closed" sign to "Open" and leaned back in his chair to get comfortable. Lita walked in and came up to his desk.

His initial surprise gave way to anger, hurt and a million other bittersweet emotions. He hardened his face and gave her a cold stare; his hands remained crossed behind his head. She was so beautiful. He still wanted her despite her betrayal. She was dressed in her uniform from the travel agency. The navy blue looked great against her honey-colored skin.

"Rolle, we have to talk," she said. He did not reply.

Behind her, Gina and Inga walked into the office and lined up behind Lita.

What do they want? He thought. Lita continued to coax him to come over to her place later, but his attention was divided. Gina and Inga were both acting bizarre. Now they were both licking stamps and trying to snatch them from each other. What in the world?

He ordered Lita to leave so he could deal with his customers. He was gratified to see the affront on her face. He was almost grateful for the distraction the two women were causing, as it helped him keep his emotions under control.

Lita left, and both Gina and Inga charged his desk. They were almost incoherent. Gina dumped a soggy ball of paper on his desk. He stared at the remnants of the sheets of stamps with disbelief. What kind of collector did this? The redhead Inga stood next to Gina staring at him eagerly. A few hours before he would have welcomed such a stare from her, but he knew this wasn't about him at all.

"More, I need more stamps, please," Gina's German accent was more pronounced and her voice shook. Her eyes seemed to be stuck in a wild, wide-eyed glare. Inga tried to smile but he was repulsed by the red foam gathered at the corners of her mouth. It looked like she had made her tongue bleed with paper cuts. Rolle was un-nerved but he figured he could handle two women, crazy as they might be.

"Ladies," he began using his reasonable voice, "Each collector is to be issued one sheet. As you know, these are first editions and they are supposed to be a limit per collector."

Inga slammed the flat of her palm on his desk, startling everyone.

"I need more!" she shouted, her voice cracking.

Rolle had had enough. He picked up his security phone and paged Arthur, the guard on afternoon duty. By now, Gina and Inga had become physical, trying to wrestle with him. He was in a dilemma. He didn't believe in hitting women, but they were trying to scratch him. Gina was a short, chubby woman but Inga had some muscle to her and he had to be a bit more firm with her. His co-workers tried to intervene but there was no reasoning with the women. By now everyone was over the humor of seeing Rolle embarrassed, and was genuinely concerned.

Rolle pushed Gina away roughly and Agnes and Joyce tried to hold her back. Arthur finally showed up looking irritated at having his nap interrupted, but quickly assessed the situation and ran to help Rolle deal with Inga.

Mr. White remained seated behind his desk quietly observing the scene. He picked up the phone and asked the operator to call the police, and then he asked her for an outside line and called the minister responsible for his department.

The police arrived in a remarkably short time. Arthur was still trying to restrain Inga, while Agnes and Joyce held onto Gina. Both were crying and screaming hysterically. Rolle stood propped up against the wall with his arms crossed over his chest, trying to make sense out of the madness.

Mr. White came out of his office as the police arrived, walked over to Rolle and spoke to him quietly. Rolle looked down his nose at his employer then went to fetch the balance of the stamps as his supervisor requested. There were five manila envelopes that had gone unclaimed so far. White returned to his office followed closely by Rolle.

White took the sheets and put them into a draw in his desk, while Rolle rubbed at the tension in his neck.

"Something is wrong with those stamps," Rolle said bluntly.

White's eyes skewered him over his glasses.

"Are you trying to suggest that the mania of these tourists was caused by stamps?" His voice dripped with scorn.

Rolle was not deterred, "They were fine until they started licking them, then they just went nuts! It's like they were on drugs or something." he said. White sat down and picked up a pen. He tapped the point on his desk for a few minutes.

"Have you written that letter for Mr. Woods?"

Rolle shook his head with disbelief,

"You can't tell me something weird isn't going on. I'm going to find out what it is." He jabbed a finger in White's direction.

He went back to his desk looking for the sheet of stamps he had hidden away. He had planned to sell it privately but now had serious doubts. He let it lie in the drawer and stared at the colorful prints. The plumage of the bird was bright blue and green. In fact, it was like no bird he had ever seen on St. Marts, not that he knew much about local birds. He suddenly became aware that he had taken it out of the drawer and was slowly bringing it closer to his mouth. He dropped it in shock and shut the drawer quickly, looking to see if anyone had noticed. He wiped his forehead as he tried to remember taking the sheet from the drawer. He was sweating profusely and felt nauseous. It was frightening. He locked up early at 3:30 p.m. and went into the cafeteria to avoid White's scrutiny.

Arthur the guard was in the cafeteria relating the earlier drama to some of the workers who had missed the action. When Rolle walked in Arthur called him to join the conversation.

"Rolle, man, come and tell them about the crazy ladies, they think I'm making it up."

Rolle grabbed a cold juice from the fridge and paid the cash out to the cafeteria lady.

He wanted some time to think through the events of the day, but Arthur continued to press him until he corroborated the story. Of course, in Arthur's version, the women were possessed by devils, and fighting with supernatural strength.

Rolle stayed out of it, mostly amused by the grand re-telling. The workers exclaimed as Arthur waved his hands in the air, and described how the women had tried to throw him across the room.

"And I tell myself, what! No devil stronger than me, so I grab one and I hold her down," his said, his face contorting comically as the others burst out laughing.

Sonia, the cafeteria lady left the cash register and sat down next to Rolle.

"But, you know, I heard about this before," she said. He glanced at her sharply.

"What you mean?" he asked.

"Arthur? Remember about three years back? In one of the village branches? A Swiss scientist from EverGreen Labs was going mad in the post office. They deported him or something?" She looked at Arthur who pursed his lips thoughtfully.

"I think so... but that's a different thing man. He wanted a certain kind of stamp and it was a limited edition. This is a different thing," Arthur said and went back into his tale. Sonia shrugged and got up. She began wiping off the tables.

Not so different at all, Rolle thought to himself. Arthur didn't know about the stamps he had given to Gina and Inga. Maybe he was being paranoid. He left work still feeling disoriented and walked alone to Scorpio Bar.

There was a madman preaching outside the Bar, the one everybody called the Prophet. He was dressed up like Gandhi in khaki-coloured robes wrapped around his body. He wasn't dirty per se, just worn out and sun dried. Still, Rolle kept a wide berth of him. The Prophet was upset with the bar's proprietors and patrons, ranting about the demons of liquor. Rolle tried to slip inside while the Prophet's back was turned, but the Prophet's uncanny sixth sense made him swing around and block the door with the staff he carried. Rolle stopped short. He wasn't up to fighting more mad people.

The Prophet's long locks hung from beneath a khaki turban. His eyes were red and his stare was compelling.

"Neither rain nor sleet nor snow must stop the pony express," the Prophet recited with earnest seriousness.

Rolle couldn't help himself, he burst out laughing; his first real laugh in days. The Prophet seemed perturbed and drew himself up with wounded pride. He saluted Rolle formally, his body ramrod straight. Rolle couldn't stop laughing. The tension of the day was released in floods. The Prophet remained at attention, his arm still in salute. Rolle decided he had enough fun at the poor man's expense and turned to go inside the Bar. The madman's words stopped him cold.

"Mr. Postman you must stop selling the foreign poison, sir!" The Prophet dropped his hand and saluted sharply again, knocking his hard bare heels together. Rolle stood still, an uncertain smile still playing on his lips.

"What?" he asked. The Prophet acted like he was reporting to a commanding officer.

"I have seen them on the mountain, the foreign white devils making their poison." He focused his fierce gaze on Rolle and in true mad man style became enraged for no apparent reason. He pointed his staff at Rolle and shouted, "You, sir, are guilty of dereliction of duty!"

Rolle went into the Bar annoyed at himself for being drawn into that embarrassment. He should have known better as it was not the first time or even the second time he had encountered the Prophet. When he'd been a child, the Prophet was someone he and his schoolmates teased from a respectful distance. The madman was like Moses or Elijah in the Bible spouting fire and brimstone. But on rare occasions, like today, he would sound as though he was privy to some great secret, and there would be a flash of clarity in his tirade.

Rolle was mildly surprised when Agnes sat down beside him and ordered a drink. She was eager to talk about incident with Gina and Inga. As they talked, Rolle began to speculate about the stamps. Some kind of new drug? Did that explain why he himself had been entranced when he examined the sheet? He still could not recall taking it out of the drawer.

Do I really want to know? He wondered.

Agnes's voice broke into his reverie, "White has never given out free stamps to tourists before. I wonder why he started now?" she mused.

"What about the International Philately Society? Isn't that normal for registered members?" Rolle reminded her. She frowned.

"What society? We don't have any philately society," she said.

At that point an impulse came over him to return to the office and get the stamps out of his drawer. He told Agnes he had forgotten something and left the Bar. The Prophet shouted after him that wine was a mocker.

Rolle jogged back to the post office, and convinced a reluctant Arthur to let him in. As he expected, the office was deserted but he thought he heard a murmur from White's office. Just to be sure Rolle quietly padded across the room and put his ear to the closed door. He could hear White on the phone.

"…shouldn't be a problem now. The reaction was much faster than we had anticipated. Uh-huh…We should stick to the rural districts, where we can contain the gossip much easier. Too many college types around here," White barked a laugh.

The other party on the phone spoke at length for some time then Rolle heard White say something that shook him.

"He won't be a problem. We're getting rid of him. He's been overcharging the collectors and pocketing the extras."

Rolle jerked in surprise. No doubt who "he" was. He thought he'd been careful, not taking too much at a time. He could still hear White quite clearly.

"Yes, they were taken to the Psych unit but have been moved to the Lab for further observation."

There was the sound of paper rustling and then White's voice sharpened.

"I don't care what they want. We can't risk such a public display again. I'm sending these things back to the Lab first thing in the morn..." White's voice trailed off.

Rolle, still standing outside the door, knew exactly what was happening. White had opened the envelope and realized there was a sheet of stamps missing.

Poison stamps, the phrase came to his mind.

White would get up and take his keys to Rolle's desk. There was no time for Rolle to get out before White would be out of his chair. He could take White easily in a physical contest, but he figured he was up against something way more sinister than White. It all flashed through his head in a matter of seconds.

He heard White's curse as he hurriedly ended the conversation and put down the phone. There was only one way to play this. Rolle moved quickly and roughly pushed White's door open. It slammed into the wall. Then he leaned against the door jamb insolently and crossed his arms. He even smiled.

To say White was startled would be an understatement. He was frozen, half out of his chair looking like he had been caught red-handed which was exactly what Rolle wanted.

White, however, recovered quickly.

"Mr.Trelfor...I assume you're breaking into my office for a good reason?" He sat down and shuffled papers as though he was tidying up to leave.

"I know what you're doing," Rolle kept his tone smooth and confident. White's eyes gleamed as he assessed Rolle.

"No you don't," he responded equally confident.

Rolle smiled broadly.

White's gaze narrowed.

Rolle tried another tactic. He was glad he was leaning on the door jamb because he could feel a line of sweat running down his back.

"You want those stamps back, right?"

White's gaze did not waver.

Rolle uncrossed his hands and flexed his still bruised knuckles.

"It's sick what you're doing to those people. You drugging them."

He cracked his knuckles as though he could not wait to use them.

White leaned back in his chair and picked up his ball point pen. He tapped the nib on the desk so hard it would never work again.

"Mr. Trelfor, I think your particular skills are not being utilized in the Philately department. We have an opening coming up that I believe would interest you."

Rolle never took his eyes off White.

"I'm not interested in working in some village," he said.

White's face was expressionless.

"No, I have something here in mind, where we could work closely… collaborate on projects as they arose."

And you can keep an eye on me, Rolle guessed.

He was unsure of what he wanted to do. His instinct told him to quit and get as far from the Post Office as possible, but the opportunity to make it big was unfolding. He thought of his father finally being proud of him. He thought of Lita seeing him in his expensive cars and suits, and mourning over what she had thrown away. He thought of his mother too, but she would want him to do the right thing, like call the police. He instinctively knew that would do no good. Who knew how high up this went? White was obviously not top dog of whatever it was Rolle had stumbled into.

"Make me an offer and make it good," Rolle injected as much arrogance as he could into the demand.

In the end, he called Andre to work out the deal for him. Andre was coolly professional although obviously uncomfortable with the strange contract. He also wasn't pleased at having to sign a confidentiality agreement.

Rolle refused to give back the stamps to White. Instead he gave them to Andre who agreed to secure the mysterious envelope. Not even Rolle knew where they were hidden, but of course White would never know that.

Rolle received his own office on the third floor of the post office, with a splendid view of the boulevard and the marina. He brought his father to see it, and was gratified when the old man shook his hand and congratulated him. Agnes was mystified and annoyed he had become her senior. She redoubled her efforts to seduce him.

In the years that followed, he monitored the office gossip for news about tourists behaving strangely in the out districts, but it never happened again.

In the meantime, he kept an eye on White, and White kept an eye on him.

8. Sacrifice

As he struggled to lift the goat into the back of his luxurious SUV, City Councilor Peter Woods sweated. His vehicle was the only one of its kind on St. Marts and he was very proud of it. Only five more years of payments to the bank and it would be all his, but nobody need know about that.

The goat was pungent and it left a faint trace of poop on his jacket sleeve. He swore at the animal and managed to get it to stay put, tying its piece of homemade, rope leash to an empty gas cylinder he kept forgetting to take back to the gas station. He hoped the animal would not get strangled if he took a corner too sharply, or bumped on the rough terrain he planned to travel. He glanced about him quickly but there was no sign of any cars coming either way on the highway.

Sunday afternoons tended to pass quietly in this particular area. He took off his jacket that now stank of sweat and feces, and tossed it in the passenger seat. He really should throw it away, so there would be no evidence. But nobody had seen him, and why would anyone think he would steal a goat? Plus the jacket was expensive.

He sped, heading north for another five minutes along the coast until he came to a small village that consisted of twenty houses or so. He turned off the highway and into the village, navigating the rocky, narrow dirt roads with difficulty. Most of the villagers were relaxing inside their homes watching television, but a few were out on their verandas. They waved in greeting as he drove past. He drove up to the end of a one way road that disappeared into the forest. It was one of those scenarios where the government had simply run out of money for road works, and let the road be reclaimed by nature. He parked on the end of the paved street just where the grass and vines began, and got out.

There was only one small wooden hut, a few feet up a little hill behind the wall of trees and bush. He glanced around him. There were two old men playing dominos on the verandah. They studiously ignored him as they played.

He tried not to feel self-conscious. It wasn't as if people didn't know that he came to see Marshall. He wasn't the only politician who had come here to seek… advice; however, he had never come in daylight before, and somehow the sunshine seemed like a spotlight on him and on the Pathfinder. He wished the old men would go inside, and let him at least have the illusion he wasn't being spied on. He went to the back of the truck and retrieved the goat. It had made a small mess in the back, and he could have cheerfully killed it right then and there.

He struggled again as he made a little hop over the small river between the paved road and the earth bank, and walked up the hill behind the veil of trees.

Marshall, was attending to plants in his garden. He looked up and his bushy, white eyebrows flew up for an instant when he saw the goat.

"Why you carrying the goat?" Marshall's harsh, gruff voice sounded extra loud.

"Well, I…I thought it would try to run away," Peter said haplessly as he really looked for the first time at the leash. Feeling silly, he put the goat down and took the leash in his hand. He tugged experimentally and the goat followed. Marshall humphed, and went into the small hut, carrying the hoe he had been using in his garden. The goat was very interested in the green leaves poking out of the soil, but Peter did not dare let it nibble; no telling how angry Marshall might get or what he might do. He moved closer to the door of the hut and looked in.

Marshall seemed to have forgotten all about him. He was sitting at his little wood table peeling vegetables, then spoke without looking up from his tanias.

"You know what to do. When you finish come back to me. Don't do it too close to my house, I don't want to have no mess to clean up."

Peter knew he was not referring to the goat's manure.

Killing the goat was hard. It wasn't smooth going as he expected. It twitched convulsively even after he was done. Although he had often made goat soup as a teen, he was now sickened by the smell. He felt people were spying on him from behind the trees. He performed the ceremony and whispered his desire to the wind.

What does it profit a man to gain the whole world and lose his soul? His mother's words came to his mind.

He shrugged off the guilt as he buried the entrails the way Marshall had told him to. Fortunately, there was a small river flowing nearby so he bathed as best as he could. The cold water revived him, made his body tingle and gave him a renewed energy. He walked back to Marshall's hut wearing his underwear, and carrying his neatly wrapped up dress shirt and pants under his arm.

Marshall was cooking a broth of smoked meat and vegetables that looked hearty and smelled delicious. He did not offer any to Peter.

"Where did you get that goat?" Marshall asked. Peter pulled on his pants, reached into his pant pocket and took out five new one hundred dollar bills and dropped them on the little wood table.

"On the side of the road coming here," he responded, feeling it was no point lying to Marshall who seemed to know everything anyway.

Marshall picked up the bills and put them into an old Danish butter cookie tin. Peter noted it seemed to be quite full already. He left Marshall with a sense of resignation. One day he might have to give up more than money for what he had purchased, but maybe that was years away still.

The next day Peter Woods and his wife smiled, and posed for pictures for the newspapers before they went into the little booth, and cast their votes against the incumbent mayor Lloyd Johnson. Peter made the rounds at the rum shops and hang out spots, shaking hands, making promises and bad jokes. In the evening, he stayed home listening to the radio; waiting for the news...*his* news, to come on at 6:00p.m.

His wife wondered at his unusually relaxed demeanor. Normally, he would be filled with an angry tension that would explode into ranting and raving as the inevitable loomed. Today he actually lay quietly on the sofa, hands crossed over his stomach, smiling to himself. The announcer made a corny joke and she was shocked to hear Peter's answering chuckle. Maybe he was finally dealing with his annual disappointment like a man for once. This seemed unlikely, so she decided it was more prudent to find some errand outside the house to do, and left him alone with his radio.

Finally the sounds of the news theme song trumpeted and there were three exquisite seconds of anticipation before the anchor announced that …incumbent mayor Lloyd Johnson had been re-elected for the 12th time, in a landslide victory.

Peter sat, shocked and disbelieving, before he grabbed the radio and slammed it against the wall.

At about the same time, Marshall was sitting on his verandah playing dominos as he listened to the results. Of course he wasn't surprised. Lloyd Johnson had paid him one thousand dollars weeks earlier. His domino partner cocked an ear as the headlines were read.

"Eh Marsh, look like your boy Peter Woods lose out again," he said with a grin.

Marshall's eyes stayed on the dominos.

"That's what you get for thiefing my goat," he replied.

9. The Prophet

Robert Windsor dreamed as he floated in the immersion tank. He couldn't feel the sensors that had been attached to his head and limbs, but the tightness of the air mask over his nose and mouth, bothered him. He frowned, and a voice echoed in his ear.

"It's ok Robert, you're doing fine," the soothing female voice said, and he relaxed.

He slipped into a dream where he walked barefoot on a paved road that led to the entryway of the St. Frances National Gardens. He stopped at the gates feeling a familiar dissonance.

There should be white wooden gates here, not wrought iron ones, he thought. He could remember that even before the white gates, there had been miles of cane fields. Even in his dreams, his mind struggled to sift through the memories of many eras. There had been horses, and a white house overlooking the fields.

I remember the sweat in my eyes and the sting of the whip on my back.

His body jerked in the tank, and the doctor who was monitoring his vitals made a signal to her assistants that it was time to end the session.

Dr. Ashla Lewis glanced at the man in the tank. His mass of locks floated all around him like tentacles. His eyes remained closed but his forehead creased deeper. She took some notes to keep her mind on the job, and tried to ignore the armed guard in the far right corner of the lab. Beneath her concentration, an undercurrent of fear knotted her stomach.

Her patient was removed from the tank and dressed in freshly laundered robes. She watched bemused, as the lab assistants deferentially wrapped the khaki robe around his emaciated frame. The irony amazed her. Robert Windsor was perhaps the most abused specimen of EverGreen Labs and yet he was revered as a king. One of the assistants wrapped a turban of the same khaki material around Robert's head, allowing his locks to hang down his back. The matted hair of his scalp covered over the criss-cross of scars from numerous incursions into his brain. He stood before them with a mute dignity. The poignancy of the moment as they stood back and surveyed him moved her, and she wiped sudden tears from behind her glasses

She gave him a sedative, hardening her heart to the myriad tracks on his arm. She eased him gently into a lying position on a cot. Dr. Stowebridge, the head of the Lab, expected results not morals.

"How are you feeling Robert?" she asked to begin the conversation. Maybe conversation was too technical a term. He rambled on and she listened, just as all her predecessors had, and took down the few lucid thoughts that emerged through the colourful imagery.

Robert Windsor's files were long and detailed. Stowebridge had once showed her the earliest records they had on him; yellowed, dog-eared paper files that smelled of mildew. They dated back to the Lab's first year of operation in 1906.

Robert spoke in a hoarse voice, alternating between colloquialism and standard English. Despite her troubled thoughts, Ashla listened with a familiar sense of awe. The things he had seen were beyond belief. His mere presence was impossible.

The secrets of the island of St. Marts were locked away in his fevered brain, but how to get at them? Stowebridge had cursed the barbarism of the early EverGreen directors. She claimed that Robert had once been intelligent, lucid and even a teacher at the prominent St. Frances Boys School, before the experimental surgeries.

Ashla stared at his sunbaked skin, at the wrinkles at the corners of his eyes and the thin skin of his hands. Even with the effects of living out under the elements, he could pass for a middle-aged man.

"It's not time to sleep," he said and turned his gaze from the overhead lights to look at her. She caught her breath. Robert was in one of those golden moments; in his right mind.

"Yes?" she coaxed gently, trying not to let her voice betray her eagerness.

"They want me to sleep, but it's not time. I don't feel 'Her' communing with me."

His cadence and grammar were now almost as British as Stowebridge's, the result of a Victorian era teacher's training.

Ashla thought rapidly. If she could show Stowebridge she'd been able to get new information from him, maybe she could buy more time. Her life depended on it.

"She? You mean St.Marts?" she prompted.

He looked at her sternly, "St.Martin," he corrected, giving the French pronunciation.

Ok. This was good. It wasn't new information but at least she had a handle on what they were talking about.

"You slept, I mean "She" told you to sleep…the last time was before the Earthquake of 1762?" Ashla said as she scrolled through the notes on the tablet quickly.

He was silent and his face impassive, but then she was alarmed to see tears begin to gather in the corners of his eyes.

"A big storm threatened so I felt the urge to sleep. I told my woman and son we could hide in the cave on this mountain. Everyone on the plantation was busy nailing down the doors and windows on the great house, so we took the chance to escape. I knew the dogs were locked up so we crawled through the cane fields," his voice was heavy with sorrow.

Ashla let out a breath of frustration. Not the 1762 Earthquake then, but the Hurricane of 1679.

"The sky was black, riotous," he continued, "My son was afraid but I comforted him. I told him the island would protect us," he said.

He fell silent for a few moments.

"When I woke up, my wife and little boy were long gone. Everything had changed," he shuddered as sobs shook his body.

She touched his hand in pity.

"How do you know when it's time to sleep?" she asked, hoping to change his mood.

He raised a shaking hand to his face and wiped his tears.

"I told you. She tells me when it's time. I am 'Her' child."

He swallowed hard. Ashla gripped his bony hand. This was getting her nowhere.

She had a sudden thought.

"I was born here too, so am I 'Her' child?" she suggested.

His deep set dark eyes focused on her thoughtfully.

"You born here, yes, but you not born of 'Her' spirit. You not her child," he said with an apologetic look.

"I want to help you, Robert," she said, trying not to panic. His vocabulary and cadence had begun to change. She was losing him.

He sat up in a swift movement, startling her. She heard the rustle of the guard changing positions. Robert covered her hand with his own.

"She always protect me, lady. Is you who going to die," he said counting his words like he was speaking to a dull child.

Ashla felt the blood drain from her face but she believed him. He was after all, the Prophet.

"Why?" she asked softly.

"The Americans always hide the Lab when they ready, and they kill to keep the secrets," he said. His eyes pitied her.

He suddenly made a growl and she snatched her hand away.

"Fire and brimstone! Judgment and death!" he yelled, fixing her with his typical fierce stare.

The Prophet was back. Time to turn him loose.

At first she had been perplexed that he was allowed to roam through town so freely but soon realized there was no threat. He shouted his dire warnings in the streets, amidst a people who no longer saw or heard him. He was just a madman.

She stood up and took off the blood pressure cuff from his arm, and spoke urgently under her breath, "Go to the police. Tell them what's happening here. Do you understand?"

"Hell fire and divine wrath," Robert responded. She despaired as she looked at him. His pupils were almost fully dilated.

He stood up, his bare feet hitting the cold floor. He walked past her, out of the office and to the main double doors. The guard swiped a security card and the door slid open for a brief moment. The Prophet went out and she stared longingly at the lit hallway, catching a glimpse of the freedom that lay beyond the doors.

Her eye was caught by a flicker of movement from the guard. He was fingering the trigger of his weapon absently.

10. Scorpio's

Retired Police Chief Dunstan George, sat in the sunken room of Scorpio's Bar and observed the patrons. It was so much cooler here, with its stone walls, and rough concrete floor, compared to the sticky humidity outside. He was comfortable, leaning back against the leatherette seat of the tiny booth. With his fingers laced across his midsection, he watched people push past the crush of bodies in the entryway to get into the bar. He saw Rolle Trelfor come in around 11:00 p.m, and head straight to the counter.

"Mr. Trelfor, the usual?" Scorpio's strident voice cut through the loud, chatter. He gave Rolle a full bottle of rum. Rolle took the bottle and walked over to Dunstan's booth, and sat across the small table from him.

"Goodnight, Chief," Rolle said as he put two shot glasses on the table.

A shout rose from another corner across the bar, as domino tiles were slapped onto wooden table tops with vigor. Rolle poured two shots from the bottle of white rum which contained some dark green leaves.

"Here's to you, Chief. I plan to get very drunk tonight," Rolle announced, downing the shot.

Dunstan took a cautious sip from his own glass and grimaced. The taste was herbal and the alcohol was potent. He glanced at Scorpio who was chatting to a customer, his sunburnt face wreathed with pungent smoke from his cigar.

Scorpio caught his eye and stepped out from behind the bar to come to their booth. Dunstan coughed and Scorpio quickly whisked the cigar out of his mouth.

"Sorry, Chief, just celebrating my new grandson," he explained, exposing his yellow teeth in a grin.

"Congratulations," Dunstan replied in tribute to the achievement, "Could we get some black coffee? Strong as you can make it."

Scorpio glanced at Rolle, winked at Dunstan, and returned to the bar. Rolle poured out another shot for himself, and Dunstan watched the particles settle to the bottom of the bottle to rest with other sediment. Rolle threw back the shot, letting its fiery contents blaze its way to his stomach.

"Ay boy," he winced. He turned his attention to Dunstan.

"You felt the tremor this morning? Around 5:00a.m. or so? I hear Red Cross planning more evacuation drills," he said.

Dunstan grunted assent. There had been several strong tremors over the last month. It was worrying.

"I heard you resigned as Postmaster General," he answered, getting to the point.

Rolle's shoulders drooped and he drummed his fingers on the table for a few minutes, then he straightened up and laughed lightly.

"Well, now Minister Peter Woods is in office, it was suggested I take early retirement. He doesn't like me too much," Rolle replied.

"Why not?"

"I once knocked him to the ground when he was giving out flyers," Rolle chuckled.

"When was this?"

"Oh, about five years ago."

"Holds a grudge, eh?"

As Rolle languidly traced a circle around the big "D" on the bottle's label, the table began to sway and Dunstan frowned. Perhaps Rolle was rocking the unsteady base with his foot? But Rolle also looked surprised. The shaking lasted for a minute before the lights went out. Groans greeted the black-out but Scorpio shouted he had kerosene lamps and to just hold tight, which was met with loud cheering.

They sat in silence, feeling the dark enveloping them like a suffocating cloak.

"I wish I could leave St.Marts," Rolle said suddenly.

Scorpio lit a large hurricane lamp, casting a warm, amber glow over the bar.

"What's stopping you?" Dunstan asked.

Rolle's expression became wary. Dunstan regarded him. There it was again; that caution Rolle always seemed to have.

"Unfinished business," Rolle said. He drained another shot.

Dunstan waited. Rolle suddenly slapped his palm on the table.

"Five years….five years! And I still don't understand!" he continued, obviously aggrieved.

Dunstan listened as Rolle stammered out a bizarre story, about a conspiracy to give drugged stamps to two European tourists.

"I found out later they both died. The news said it was a drug overdose," Rolle sighed. He couldn't seem to meet Dunstan's gaze.

Dunstan felt the hairs rise on the back of his neck. This was not just drunken rambling.

He stared at Rolle's bowed head as he reflected. Strange things always happened on St. Marts: Unsolved murders and so-called accidents. There were legends of monsters, and areas in the mountains and forests where no one ventured. His own daughter-in-law had gone mad, run into the bush, and could not be found. Not be found…on an island!

A man walked over to their table.

"You want a game Chief?" he asked. He held a pack of dominos in his left hand and a beer bottle in his right.

"Not right now, Sonny, but you'll join us?"

Sonny nodded, put the pack on the table and looked around for a spare stool. Some of the bar patrons had left because of the black out, so he found one immediately.

"How's that situation in your neighbourhood?" Dunstan asked.

A muscle jumped in Sonny's jaw, and then he took a long swig of his beer. Dunstan called out to Scorpio for another shot glass.

"Rolle, you might find this interesting," Dunstan indicated to Sonny, who absently scratched at a scar of two holes about an inch apart, on one of his muscular forearms.

Sonny hesitated, and then began speaking in a low voice they had to strain to hear. He told a tale about his neighbours being spiders or witches. And then Dunstan told his story about children with altered bodies who were gifted athletes, but died young. And Rolle once again shared about the things that had happened in his post office five years before. Then they told the strange stories that they had heard from a friend of a friend, and the night wore on in this fashion. The stories dated back generations. Some stories they laughed at, but eventually they sat in silence.

"It all comes back to the Lab, have you noticed?" Dunstan said, referring to the American based facility. It was a mysterious place. People in town gossiped about the strange lights, noises and even human experiments rumoured to take place there. But there had never been any proof. Rolle accepted his statement in silence, but Sonny shrugged.

Scorpio shut up the bar around 1:00a.m., half an hour past the legal time to serve alcohol in town. Dunstan ignored this.

"Hey, full moon," Sonny observed as they stepped into the quiet street.

Most of the town was shut down except for the odd rum shop like Scorpio's. They stared up at the ivory orb whose brilliance illuminated the distant hills. The sound of crickets chorused around them.

"What's that smell?" Rolle asked with a screwed up face.

Dunstan noticed the sulphorous reek in the air as well. He looked over his shoulder to see if they were near a garbage skip, and jumped. A man was standing right behind him.

It was the madman, the Prophet.

Rolle said in a gentle voice, "Good night, cousin."

The Prophet glanced at Rolle, but his fevered gaze flicked back to Dunstan.

"Police…is you I come for," he rasped.

"What can I do for you?" Dunstan asked.

The Prophet's mouth worked soundlessly and his eyes rolled back in his head. He staggered a few steps towards Dunstan and swayed. Dunstan grabbed his arm to keep him steady. In the moonlight, Dunstan noticed numerous needle tracks on the Prophet's forearm.

"You must come and stop them," the Prophet urged.

Angry tears filled the vagrant's eyes and disappeared into his unkempt beard. He made a swiping motion at Dunstan who ducked, but stood his ground.

"Them who?" Rolle asked.

Dunstan was puzzled. The Prophet was troublesome, but the needle tracks in his arms were surprising. Marijuana, yes, but hard drugs?

"Lab," the Prophet said and looked over his shoulder furtively.

"EverGreen Labs?" Dunstan's interest was instantly engaged.

"You know man!" The Prophet grew agitated.

Sonny interjected, "You can't get in that place. Their security real tight."

Rolle, who must have been feeling warm with rum and love for his fellow man spoke up.

"You coming home with me, cousin," he said.

The Prophet shook his head.

"Police, I take you up there," The Prophet turned his intense gaze on Dunstan.

"You know you can't get in there just like that," Sonny insisted, "They got security guards, guns and everything."

The Prophet's wild eyed stare made Dunstan wonder if he ever blinked.

"Tomorrow night, meet me on the main road to the Morn. I show you a way in," The Prophet said, sounding lucid.

Dunstan wondered how seriously he should take this.
I've been trying for eleven years to get in there to investigate, and now, out of nowhere...is this really my chance? He pondered.
Sonny argued for a few more minutes that it was impossible to get in, regardless of what the Prophet said. The Prophet became enraged.

"You must come, police!"

He jabbed at Dunstan's ample midsection as he yelled, "People will die!"

The three men stared at him dumfounded. He was truly mad.
Dunstan put his hand on the vagrant's shoulder and looked him in the eye.

"I coming, ok? Tomorrow night."

The Prophet's face twitched and his eyes bulged. He turned his head sharply towards the road, which sloped behind them and stared down the empty, dark street. Suddenly, he turned and ran up the road ahead of them, slipped down a side alley and out of sight.

They all turned at the sound of a car coming up the road behind them. A white van with tinted glass drove slowly past them. The three men saw the big green EG logo emblazoned on the side. They watched, bemused, as it continued its slow ascent up the road.

"You think…they looking for him?" Rolle asked.

Sonny glanced at Dunstan whose eyes were glued to the vehicle.

"You really going, Chief?"

Dunstan, never took his eyes off the van, "Definitely."

The next morning, Dunstan sat in his small office of the St. Marts National Sports Board shuffling through paperwork. Admitting to himself that he was too distracted to work, he unlocked a lower draw on his desk, and took out the files that had become so precious to him.

He turned the pages in the first file, and let his fingers rest on the photograph of a young woman dressed in a graduate cap and gown. Eleven years had passed since he had watched her swim to the horizon and vanish before his eyes. Eleven years…her parents had gone to their graves with no answer as to how and why their daughter had died. That was his fault. The others were his fault too. He had found more of them, these star children. He had attempted to take them under the wing of the National Sports Board, provide training, schooling, mentorship. Some had gone on to various levels of success in their sport, but others had dropped out along the way.

Those others were in these files. He stared at the stack. His anger had long been displaced by bitterness. He couldn't save the ones who didn't pursue whatever manifest destiny they had been designed for. They all died under mysterious circumstances.

The smoky aroma of meat grilling wafted through his window. He had asked for an office away from the St. Frances city center, and so was in a small, three bedroom house that had been bought cheap when the German owners turned Rasta and took off to the bush. The Sports Board wasn't high up on the list of government priorities, so with no budget to renovate, he had enlisted the help of some of his former subordinates on the Force and done the work himself. It had turned out well. His own space was painted sky blue, and he was fortunate enough to have a view of the beach on the other side of the road.

It was restful to watch the turquoise waves, the anchored fishing boats, and the little wood hut where that fisherman with all the kids lived. The children were especially wonderful to watch; they played with such excitement and abandon. Good looking bunch too with their sun bleached locks. He often wondered how such a thin, dried out man had produced such vital, beautiful offspring. There didn't seem to be a mother around, which was a pity.

The main door was open to allow in breeze and the smell of salt from the sea. A rotund woman carrying a package wrapped in foil knocked on the door, and entered.

"Lunchtime, Chief," she grinned and waddled in.

He slowly got out his wallet and hoped he had exact change. Myrtle was apt to forget to bring him back his change when he gave her larger bills. He tutted as he realized he'd used up his coins at Scorpio the night before. He pursed his lips as he handed over the twenty, and Myrtle received it cheerfully.

"I haven't sell much yet so I'll bring the change this afternoon, ok?" she promised.

"Humph, yeah right," he said.

"Don't say that, Chief, you make people think I crooked!" Her plump face expressed a dramatic horror that quickly slid back to her usual cheeky grin.

"Yes, yes," Dunstan waved her away, wondering why grown men were afraid to cross him, and this fat granny had no problem cheating him.

"Myrtle…what do people say about the Lab, these days?" he asked on impulse. Myrtle's thick eyebrows shot up and she shrugged.

"Not much, Chief. The Americans have the place lock up, and have guard all around. They almost shoot some boys the other day because they were climbing the mango trees just outside the big fence…imagine little school boys like that," she shook her head in disgust.

"No one reported it to the police?"

"Tell police for what? What they can do? Those people have Government permission to do their thing," she replied and made a disparaging noise. He noticed she had slipped his twenty into her apron pocket, and bid it a silent farewell.

After she left, he dug into the wings, a little guilty because he was breaking Margery's dietary requirements for him, but to him the wings tasted even better because of it. He sat, thick, sweet and tangy BBQ sauce coating his fingers as he ate.

He watched the waves break gently into foam on the black shoreline across the road. The tips of the waves glittered in the noontime sunshine. Every now and again, a car would zoom down the road, interrupting his view for a brief second. Maybe that's why he didn't see when the woman on the beach appeared.

He paused with the meat in his mouth, as a woman walked out of the water and headed down the beach towards the boats and the fisherman's hut. She was very striking with long, black locks down to her thighs, and walked with the carriage of a queen. Her flawless skin shone and her figure was perfection. He registered it all, almost as much as the fact that she was completely nude. Well, she had some sort of seaweed or vine wrapped around her waist but that was it.

Dunstan dropped the wing and stared. Public nudity? Disturbing the peace? What should she be arrested for? Then he remembered yet again that he was retired. He picked up his wing and ate, his eyes glued to the amazing scene.

She disappeared into the hut, and he could almost swear he heard the screams of children over the sound of the surf. He put the wing down and pushed himself back from the desk but before he could stand up, the fisherman came running out of the hut and began untying one of the boats.

Dunstan was relieved to see the man's children also rush out and begin piling into the boat, chattering excitedly. The nude woman also came and seemed to be helping them store belongings in the small vessel. Dunstan got up and walked over to the window and leaned on the sill, licking his fingers.

None of them seemed shocked by the woman's nudity. The fisherman moved with an urgency that disturbed Dunstan's policeman's instinct. This was some kind of emergency. The fisherman and the woman pushed the boat into the water, and then the woman climbed in. The children swarmed her, hugging and talking excitedly. It was quite a charming family scene, nudity and all.

The fisherman climbed in as well. He grabbed the oars and began rowing with a steady pace. Dunstan judged that they were moving in the direction of the neighbouring island of San Martino. He wondered if the fisherman's arms would last out at the pace he was going.

Dunstan watched the boat for a bit, wondering what he had just witnessed. Then he went into the narrow bathroom and washed his hands. He needed to work on a real plan for getting into the Lab; he couldn't really expect the Prophet to show up, or even to know how to get in.

Something was wrong with his eyes. The mirror over the sink was moving. Then he realized what was happening as it shook violently and fell into the sink, shattering on impact with the ceramic bowl. He turned quickly but felt slivers stung his cheek. The whole building swayed and he put out his hands on either side of the wall as the shaking continued. Agonizing minutes passed, and he could hear shouts from outside. Sweat poured down his face and his heart thudded.

At long last, the horrendous shaking stopped. There were now several long cracks running from the ceiling, down the wall, to the floor, and bits of crumbled cement and paint dotted the tiled floor. He eased his hands away as though afraid the walls would cave in without his support.

"Chief! Chief!"

He opened the bathroom door carefully and stepped into the hallway. Myrtle was at the front door anxiously looking in, her hands wringing her apron.

"I'm ok. Anybody hurt?" He called out, and cleared his throat.

His stomach still felt a little shaky, but that feeling went away when he stepped outside and saw the damage. Cars were parked on the road haphazardly, and two drivers were yelling at each other. People were standing around, speaking to each other in frightened murmurs. Myrtle was now collecting chicken legs from the ground. Her grill was on its side and charcoal was spilled around it. Her son was pouring water over the hot coals to prevent the dry grass from catching fire.

As he surveyed the scene, Dunstan noticed an unpleasant egg-like odour in the air. He turned to look at the road again. Some of the drivers were in the process of reversing and manouevering their way around the cars that were still blocking the road. He gazed at the beach, and his mouth opened slightly. The hair on the back of his neck stood up.

The fisherman's hut was flat; utterly collapsed with its thatch roof lying a few feet away. His eyes swept the horizon looking for the boat but there was nothing to be seen. He prayed they had made it. He stared at the ruined hut and pondered the opportune timing of their leaving. The nude woman had probably saved their lives.

He stepped back into the house, examining the new cracks in the walls and trying to assess the damage. The radio he kept on his desk had gone off with the loss of electricity, so he found some double AA batteries and put them in. He tuned into the national station and stood next to the desk with his thumbs tucked into his belt.

The male announcer, sounding very somber, announced the latest report from the Disaster Preparedness office. The tremor had registered almost a 5 on the Richter scale and caused structural damage to buildings across the city. Luckily, no deaths or major injuries had been reported up to news time. Dunstan frowned as the announcer warned that due to landslides, several roads were inaccessible. He called out a list which included the Mount Frances main road.

Hmmm. No road access to Mount Fran. That made getting up to the Lab a tad more troublesome. They would have to hike all the way in. He wondered if Rolle would actually show up. The young man had been quite drunk, and on sober reflection might decide breaking into a private, and dangerous facility was not for him.

He closed the office and offered Myrtle, her son and their damaged grill a ride home. He was touched when Myrtle tried to return his twenty, but told her to keep it.

He drove into town and to the police station where everybody seemed busy responding to emergencies. He called Margery from a borrowed cell phone and assured himself that she was fine. He sat and observed the frenetic activity until he caught the eye of Inspector Aurelius. She smiled and waved him over to her desk.

"Crazy day, Chief!" she exclaimed, "You feel the tremor?"

"More like an earthquake. Yes. It caused some big cracks in my office walls."

"How about Margery?"

"Perfectly fine. She copes very well,"

She grinned at him and then grabbed up the phone as it rang. He gathered from her side of the conversation, that somebody was complaining about missing livestock that had run off during the quake. He was a little surprised to see her expression change from exasperated to grave. She made vague promises to the unfortunate farmer about looking into things and hung up.

"What's happened?" he asked.

"A farmer who lives on Morn Pelé just called. He says he can see smoke coming from the heights," she said.

His eyes narrowed.

"Bush fire?" he guessed.

She shook her head slowly, "Uh-uh. He says the air smells of sulphur."

They stared at each other for a long moment. Dunstan tapped the desk twice and sighed.

"Any new reports on those landslides on the Morn Fran road?" he asked.

"Not that I know of. The Americans haven't asked for any assistance."

"Have they ever?" he tried to sound casual.

She looked at him curiously.

"Well…no. They usually handle their own affairs."

She reached for her phone and asked the operator to connect her to the Disaster Preparedness Office. Dunstan realized that she had bigger concerns now, thanked her and went home to prepare for his incursion.

Meanwhile, in his home on Morn Fran, Dunstan's son Xavier ate quickly, and gave his own son Ronnie a little kick on his shin under the dining table. The lanky, teenager screwed up his face but laughed.

"Come on, boy! Eat up!"

Ronnie pushed his rice and salad in a circle around his plate.

"I warned you not to eat all the meat first. Now you're stuck with dry rice and grass," his father joked.

Ronnie rolled his eyes and put his fork down.

"I just want to go to bed, I'm beat," he said.

Xavier grunted but secretly he was pleased. Ronnie was shaping up to be a better than average tennis player. Xavier had actually won money betting on Ronnie's local matches, and now there was talk of a tennis scholarship at a U.S. college. Maybe the U.S Open, French Open, Wimbledon would follow. Xavier wondered how one could get a piece of that action.

"No, you should put in another hour on the court," he said to Ronnie and reached out to ruffle his son's mop of twists. He happened to glance out the glass French doors at the same time. His hand froze in midair, and his mouth gaped. Ronnie looked up puzzled, and seeing his father's expression, turned quickly to look behind him.

A large dog was standing outside the glass and looking at them. A dog, more like a wolf with brown fur and a graying muzzle, and strange, intelligent eyes, regarded them. Xavier swallowed, and very slowly lowered his hand to the table. He surreptitiously took hold of his steak knife.

Ronnie got up, pushed back his chair and walked over to the doors. Xavier made a noise of warning, as Ronnie undid the latch and opened the doors. Xavier's knuckles whitened as he gripped the knife tightly. Ronnie sank to one knee and put out his hand, palm down to the animal.

Xavier heard when the teen began to sob quietly. The wolf-like dog nuzzled the teen's outstretched hand and licked it. It edged closer to him and allowed him to embrace it. Over Ronnie's shoulder, the animal's dark eyes looked steadily at Xavier. It bared its fangs in a soundless snarl. Xavier felt his stomach drop. The animal nuzzled Ronnie's neck and made a series of little growls. Ronnie buried his face in its fur and wept. Xavier, unsure of what to do, remained in his seat. He loved the boy in his own way, and was terrified for him.

They remained like that for almost an hour, until at last Ronnie seemed to empty himself of tears. He released the dog and stood up. It stepped back, looked fearlessly into the boy's eyes, then turned and vanished into the thick bushes behind the house.

Ronnie stayed watching the spot where it disappeared for a few minutes, then, Xavier saw his back straighten. Ronnie came back into the room, closed and locked the door. He turned to Xavier, his face strong and resolute.

"We have to leave St.Marts right now!"

Xavier relaxed his death grip on the knife.

"Why, what's going on? Was that…?" He couldn't bring himself to say it.

Ronnie's tone brooked no opposition.

"Yes. She says there is danger and we must leave now."

Xavier thought about some of the debt he had accrued with several local, unsavory characters. Maybe the boy was right about St.Marts getting dangerous.

"Danger?" Xavier repeated.

"The Lab is going to come after us…for me. We must leave tonight," Ronnie insisted.

Without waiting for his father's response, Ronnie turned and left the room. Xavier watched his son's new poise, with perturbed astonishment.

11. Mount Fran

Dunstan drove up to the entrance of the main road, and parked on the shoulder. Rolle, seated in the passenger seat, looked at the concrete barricades which blocked the roughly paved road that snaked its way up Morn Fran.

"They serious about nobody going up that road," Rolle remarked.

Dunstan grunted, his eyes on his mirror as cars approached, then passed them on the adjacent highway. Dunstan glanced at Rolle. Although it was a cool night, there were beads of perspiration on Rolle's forehead.

"You ok doing this?" Dunstan asked.

Rolle snorted, "I've been waiting years for this!"

He's putting on a brave face, Dunstan realized.

The Prophet was late, or early. Dunstan realized he had absolutely no idea what time all this was supposed to happen. Dunstan stared into the dark foliage framing the entry to Morn Fran. The road leading up the Morn twisted to the right, and out of his vision. He knew it ran past several large homes, and then to a few plots of farm land in the heights. Along the way was a turn off onto an old feeder road that led to EverGreen Labs. Dunstan knew despite the presence of the wealthy residents, and the farmers, the entire mountain actually belonged to the Americans.

Car lights dipped and flashed behind them as a car pulled off the road and came to a stop. They waited as the driver came out of his car and walked up to Dunstan's window.

"Any sign of the Prophet?" Sonny asked. He held a machete in his right hand.

"Nah," Rolle replied before Dunstan could respond.

Rolle got out of the car. Sonny raised his eyebrows in inquiry at Dunstan. Dunstan patted his chest near the armpit to indicate he was also armed. He got out the car.

"What about the cars?" Rolle asked.

"If we need to make a quick getaway, better to have them here," Dunstan said.

"Maybe somebody will report them parked here," Rolle pointed out.

Dunstan paused to ponder this point.

"I have a feeling, gentlemen, that they already know we're coming," he said.

Rolle's voice rose slightly, "How do you know that?"

"That van that drove past us last night…I'm sure they saw the Prophet talking to us," Dunstan replied.

As if on cue, the foliage next to the barricades parted, and the Prophet stood before them in his mad glory.

"Police, come now," he ordered. Rolle stepped forward and ducked as the Prophet swung a wooden staff at him wildly.

"No!" he shouted. Rolle stepped back.

"No cousin. You stay safe, for your mother sake" the Prophet said. He looked at Rolle with something close to affection.

Dunstan realized their plan was not going to work. He made a decision. He reached into his shirt pocket and gave a business card to Rolle, and said, "Let Sonny take you home. If you don't hear from me by morning, call this Inspector. Tell her what's happened."

Sonny handed his machete to Dunstan without protest. Rolle stared at the card, torn with indecision.

Dunstan patted his shoulder, "It will be easier to get in if it's just one person. Go home. Take care of your family."

Dunstan walked to meet the Prophet, and followed him into the bushes.

Dunstan huffed as he chopped at the saplings and brush. It was very rough going, although the Prophet seemed to nimbly make his way through the overgrowth, long robes and all. Thank goodness for the moonlight. Dunstan heaved and spat, and leaned against a tree trying to catch his breath. It had only been an hour.

"How far?" he gasped.

Sweat poured down his face and armpits and pooled under his paunch. The salt from it burned his eyes and ran into his mouth. The Prophet turned and Dunstan could see fury on his face.

Really crazy... Dunstan wondered if he was going to have to shoot this man in self-defense.

"You get fat Police-- Babylon living," the Prophet's calm words didn't match his bulging eyes. Dunstan decided to change the topic.

"What did they do to you up there?" he asked.

"Needle and needle, every time they catch me is needle!" The Prophet almost shouted out the words.

Dunstan, instantly alert, strained to hear any movement amongst the tall, dark trees, but there was nothing other than the whistle of cicadas, and the odd scratching sound of rodents moving through the undergrowth.

"They say I am immortal," the Prophet said. Dunstan found this amusing at first.

"They cut my head, do things in my mind," he continued, pointing to his turbaned head. It suddenly occurred to Dunstan that the wrap could be disguising surgical scars, rather than being a religious statement. He felt a slow rage building. Who the hell were these people to come and experiment on St. Martians like they were animals? He thought of his Star Children.

They hiked for roughly another hour, although Dunstan could have sworn it was much longer. He was blind with sweat, and his lungs burned. He stopped and swallowed past his dry throat, as they finally reached the tall, chain link fence. They walked around the fence for some time, until they came to a gate. Dunstan noticed the whole fence was topped by barbwire. He also saw the guards resting in the shadow of the flat, concrete bunker structure of the building. As he recalled from his high school history, it had once been built as an American outpost in the 1820s, as part of an initiative under the Munroe Doctrine. It had been abandoned for long periods at a time but never left U.S. hands. Now it housed EverGreen Labs.

A guard appeared at the gate and looked at them suspiciously. His hands held his rifle loosely, but Dunstan noticed that his finger was on the trigger.

"What you doing Prophet?" the guard asked. His tone was casual but his eyes never left Dunstan.

"The white lady say bring him," the Prophet answered. Dunstan felt a stir of disquiet. Had he been set up?

The guard didn't say anything at first. He touched an ear piece then said, "Say again?"

There was a sharp click as the gate unlocked electronically and swung open. The guard raised a M16A4 assault rifle and took aim at Dunstan.

"Drop the cutlass and step in," he ordered.

Another guard came up and patted Dunstan down. They took his revolver. Dunstan cursed himself for being so naïve. He had assumed the Prophet had known of some secret way to get into the facility.

Two more guards came and marched them to a door at the back of the building. It led to a large garage where Jeeps and Land Rovers were parked, and from there they walked through several sets of electronic double doors. It reminded Dunstan of the few episodes of Star Trek he had seen.

More walking; they went down long, tunnel-like hallways and still they had not seen another soul. The Prophet appeared quite bold and seemed to know his way around. The guards were not even holding him, as they were doing to Dunstan.

I've been set up, Dunstan thought, *but why?*

At last, they walked through another white corridor that slanted down and the air was cooler, and he surmised they were below ground level. The double doors here were metal, thick and impenetrable. One of the guards stepped to one side of the doors and slid a small panel down. A beam of light shot out and scanned the guard's eye. There was a sharp click that resonated loudly and one side of the doors opened slightly.

As he stepped in, Dunstan knew he must be in the heart of EverGreen Labs. The floor was immense and there were at least five glass walled rooms, where people of in white coats were busy with computers, test tubes and beakers and other paraphernalia. It looked more like a clinic than a sinister laboratory. He felt a sense of anti-climax.

Some of the areas where walled off by thick, opaque plastic sheets. Agonized squeals and shrieks emanated from behind them. He felt goose bumps breaking out on his arms. He had been wrong to underestimate the banal layout. This was indeed a bad place.

A woman, in her late 50s, with graying hair pulled into a tight bun, walked up to them. Her hazel eyes glinted behind her glasses, and Dunstan could see she was furious. She spoke to the Prophet.

"Robert, what are we going to do with you?" She teased, in a British accent. But there was an undertone of menace in her voice.

The Prophet seemed to shrink before the petite woman, his earlier bravado gone. He craned his neck around to look at Dunstan with wild eyes.

"Police," he said, his voice cracked.

The woman turned her cold eyes on Dunstan.

"You are with the police?" she asked.

Dunstan studied her and decided to try the truth.

"Retired," he said.

She gave a quick nod.

"He wouldn't have understood that," she indicated to the Prophet, "He has a limited ability to process current events," she explained. There was a certain smugness to her that Dunstan instantly disliked.

"Save us," the Prophet mumbled and then collapsed.

Another scientist hurried forward and froze for a moment when she saw him. Dunstan's eyebrows rose sharply as he recognized her.

Ashla Lewis! What was she doing here? He thought, stunned. He glanced at the other workers and recognized a few other locals, amidst obvious foreigners. Ashla knelt next to the Prophet and took his pulse. Two of the guards came forward and picked him up by his feet and under his arms. They carried him out of Dunstan's sight behind one of the opaque sheets.

"What are you doing with him?" Dunstan demanded.

"He'll be fine, Sir. He just needs his medicine. I'll take care of it Dr. Stowebridge," Ashla said, her eyes darted from him to the British woman. He realized she was pretending not to know him. He saw the tense way she gripped her clipboard, and the desperation in her eyes.

"You're giving him drugs and experimenting on him!" he accused.

"He volunteered," Dr. Stowebridge answered. There wasn't any indication of remorse or concern. Ashla turned quickly and also disappeared behind the opaque sheet.

"How can he volunteer? He's not stable," Dunstan shrugged off the guard holding his bicep.

"He was stable, at the time he volunteered," she smiled as though pleased with her own wit.

"Why did you get him to bring me here?" Dunstan tried to keep his head despite wanting to slap the smug off her face.

Dr. Stowebridge looked surprised, "I didn't. Your presence is an unwelcome distraction. I'm just curious to know what you know, which I can see now, is nothing." She turned to go.

"You're experimenting on children, I know that," he raised his voice.

He scanned the room, noticing a large display of camera feeds on a wall, overlooking an elaborate control panel. One of the feeds was a view of the neighbouring Morn Pele´. He couldn't see smoke rising from its summit, but now he knew they were monitoring it, strange ideas began to form and flesh out in his brain. The scientist had turned back to him, and seemed to be waiting.

"You make them good at sports, but when they don't follow through, you kill them somehow," he sounded as mad as the Prophet.

"Remarkable. You have a keen mind," she looked at him with the approval one would give a trained monkey.

"Why did you kill them?" His voice broke as he thought of those lost, young lives.

"Anything that doesn't fulfill its function is useless. We were testing a theory-- pre-destiny; and we simply eliminated the failed subjects." She said.

"How do you kill them?"

He saw disappointment flash across her face.

"You seemed so promising. A device implanted in the cranium that can be operated at will."

She looked over her shoulder at the wall of screens, "I don't have time for this."

"Phosphorus? The green flash?" he asked quickly.

She looked annoyed.

"Yes. I'm afraid one of the yank techs has a theatrical nature. It helps to keep the local superstitions alive."

"But why here? Why do your..." he struggled to get the words out in his disgust, "...human experimentation on my island?" he was shouting by the time he finished.

She stared at him with disbelief. He saw comprehension dawn on her.

"You think....we made them like that? On the contrary ...these children were conceived right here by your own people. *Naturally* conceived," she added with emphasis.

She walked up to one of the opaque curtains that hung from a rack, and pulled it back to reveal rows of jars filled with fluid and specimens. Dunstan recoiled. It was like the freak show of a carnival. Human embryos that were twisted and contorted; some with fangs and pointed ears, others with their bottom halves tapered to a fish tail instead of legs, or with misshapen hands more like claws. Still others had raised spikes along their spine. Most of them were more animal than human.

"You people..." he stopped because nobody who had done this could be described as human.

She smiled.

"I see your error. We are not making creatures of your neighbours. We are here, because your neighbours *are* creatures," She explained, thrusting her thin neck forward reminiscent of a turtle. "This island is truly miraculous and bizarre, and we have been trying to study it and find out why these things happen," she waved her hand at the jars.

"You're crazy! St.Marts is just like any other island," he retorted, "I've never heard of any of these … monstrosities. I was born here. I've lived here my whole life. I was a policeman, I would have heard. I would have known," he was adamant. But within his gut he knew.

Strange things always happened on St.Marts, his own words came back to taunt him.

"I'm sure you've heard stories, even as a child," Stowebridge seemed to sense his turmoil, "The witches who suck blood; the mermaids who steal children; the strange lights on the mountains and the howling no one can explain," she said.

Yes, he had heard them. Even as a young officer, he had come across strange tracks in the forest, and teeth and bones that were neither human nor animal.

"Impossible," he protested.

She shrugged, her patience ended.

"It doesn't matter what you believe…or what anyone believes now. The facility is to be shut down. The Americans have lost patience with me," she griped, and thrust her hands into her coat pocket to punctuate her disappointment.

"What do you mean?" he asked suspiciously.

"They wanted to know the secret of the island, and if these aberrations could be used in weapon application. The answer to the latter is most likely, and to the former, I don't know."

She sighed again.

"EverGreen Labs has been here almost thirty years and we still don't know why these aberrations occur."

She looked at him suddenly.

"Do you know the secret?" she asked.

He glared at her.

"Ah…well…it's going to be over soon," she muttered. She turned her back on him, and walked over to join another scientist sitting at the console in front the wall of screens, and began giving instructions.

Ashla slipped out from behind the one of the opaque sheets, and made her way surreptitiously to Dunstan. She stood about a foot away, close enough to speak to him, but she didn't. Her eyes flickered to the guard standing next to him.

Dunstan noticed the male scientist at the console was slowly raising a lever. On one of the screens, there was live footage of Morn Pelé. He surmised it must be coming from a camera attached to a plane or a drone. The scene made his blood run cold. There was definite thick, black smoke issuing from the summit.

"Why are you watching Morn Pelé?" he asked loudly.

Dr. Stowebridge ignored him.

"Why you working for these people?" Dunstan demanded, turning his sharp glance on Ashla. He noticed contrary to the "no Locals" policy he had heard about, the guards were also islanders.

"Good money," the guard next to him answered before she could respond. He sneered as he spoke.

Dunstan glared at him, "You sell out your own people, you idiot!"

The guard grew belligerent, "Yah? We'll see how much talk you have when the volcano go off."

"You prepared to die for these people?" Dunstan jerked his head to the scientists at the console.

To his surprise the guard grinned.

"We'll be long gone. They have helicopters coming for us. They got everything organize."

Dunstan thought quickly. The Prophet's words now made complete sense to him. It was St.Marts that needed saving.

Ashla suddenly spoke to the guard in an urgent whisper, "They're lying to you! You heard what she said? They can't figure out the secret, so rather than let the island fall into other hands, they're going to kill us all, and destroy the Lab!"

Dunstan saw a muscle jump in the young guard's clenched jaw as he stared at the screens. Luckily for Dunstan, one of the screens was focused on a helipad on the Lab roof where two military helicopters were stationed. He drove Ashla's point home.

"See? Only two helicopters… no room for you fellas."

Dunstan watched the conflict of emotions play over the young man's face.

"Why are they watching Morn Pelé?" Dunstan asked Ashla.

"They're injecting pressurized fluid deep into the earth's crust, triggering tremors to cause an eruption," her voice was low and tearful.

Diabolical, he thought, appalled.

"Can it be stopped?" he asked. She shook her head slowly to his horror.

The guard was still staring at the screens. Dunstan grabbed the barrel of the guard's rifle, and pulled it upwards sharply. The younger man involuntarily pulled the trigger and it fired off a burst of three rounds at the wall of screens, spraying the scientists with broken glass. The scientist at the console slumped over; blood spreading from a wound in his back. Dr. Stowebridge screamed and cowered on the ground with her hands over her ears. Sparks popped and crackled over the smoking console. Dunstan pushed the guard backwards, grabbed the rifle, and pointed it at the British scientist.

"You moron!" She screamed at him.

The other guards, taken by surprise, aimed at Dunstan but didn't shoot. Instead, they looked at Stowebridge, awaiting her order. She screamed abuses at all of them, even throwing out racist epithets. She stood up, her chest heaving.

"Stop the eruption," Dunstan ordered.

She turned her fury on Dunstan, "There is no stopping it!"

"Get him out of here!" she ordered the guards.

"You're letting me go?" Dunstan couldn't hide his surprise. He had anticipated a bloody end.

She scoffed, "There's nothing you or anyone else can do to stop it. Go home and enjoy what's left of your life."

She practically spat out the words.

"Give me the Prophet, I mean Robert," Dunstan insisted. She looked surprised, and then an expression he couldn't define swept over her face.

"Robert will be fine. He will be safe."

He didn't know why, but he believed her.

"And her," he jerked his head towards Ashla who stood holding her clipboard like a shield. Stowebridge sneered at Ashla.

"She can leave, but she won't live long."

Ashla gave a strangled sounding gasp. Grimly, Dunstan nodded, keeping his eyes locked on the scientist. She stood, now very calm and composed, watching them back out of the lab. One of the guards opened the door and they stepped through the doors, while Dunstan covered the room with the rifle. The doors closed. Ashla quickly led the way out of the maze of hallways.

He couldn't believe it when he found himself back outside the chain link fence, facing the dark tangle of trees. Ashla collapsed onto the ground sobbing, still gripping her clipboard. He dragged her up roughly by the arm and scurried into the forest and out of sight.

She let us go because she thinks I can't stop her, he realized as they half ran, stumbling through the undergrowth. He hated to admit it but Stowebridge was probably right. It was an incredible story and government was complicit. EverGreen Labs was untouchable, but he must convince people of the imminent danger from Morn Pelé.

The import of what he had to do suddenly over-whelmed him. He stopped; the sound of his breath loud against the ominous silence. Ashla stopped too and glanced over her shoulder. The sky had lightened above their heads into a dove grey dawn.

Ashla moved closer to him and whispered something about getting back to the main road. He thought about Margery then, and it gave him the impetus to begin moving again.

The flurry of activity over the next 24 hours was a testament to his stellar reputation as a former Police Chief, and the urgent warnings of the volcanologists who were monitoring things from neigbouring San. Martino. Morn Pelé smoked, and then belched ash, as the capital of St. Frances was evacuated first. Pyroclastic flows followed spewing rock and gas as the southern villages emptied. Evacuees quickly overwhelmed boats and ferries, so even the humblest fishing vessels had to be recruited. The evacuation in the north stalled, as residents preferred to go into emergency shelters and wait out the disaster.

Three days after Dunstan and Ashla escaped the Lab, tons of hot rock, lava and ash exploded from Morn Pelé in a fast moving cloud, and raced southward, incinerating everything in its path. Ash buried EverGreen Laboratories on Mount Fran.

Deep underground in the heart of the Lab, in an artificial womb, Robert "the Prophet" Windsor slept; waiting.

A year later, the island that defied logic and science, fought back against the hardened lava and pushed tendrils of grass upwards towards the sun.

In the not too distant future…

12. SEED
To Nessa.

As Gemma's father surveyed the many rows of lush, green plants stretching heavenward, he exhaled. With his forearm, he wiped sweat from his brow and thanked the powers that this particular crop was more heat resistant than its predecessors; more pest resistant too, so this year he had spent less on expensive insecticide. The summer heat had spawned record numbers of storms this year but this crop had proved hardy. Mount Fran's earth had always been famous for its fertility, and now thanks to EverGreen Labs, all of St.Marts thrived with harvest like clockwork, year after year.

Gemma glanced at him, as she sat playing with her makeshift dolls of banana leaves. With her four fingered hands, she was still quite adept at weaving her little people creations from strips of the tough leaves. She propped up her little family of leaf people on the roots of the mango tree and smiled. The sun dappled through the leaves overhead and spotlighted the small dolls. She did have regular toys, of course, but she liked to make things. The wind fluttered the leaves above and a shushing sound filled the air. She peered up into the tall tree, and her mouth watered as she saw the sweet fruit clustered in the boughs. Most would be harvested for market but Daddy would take some home. The fruit was uniformly ripe; each one was large, golden red, and seedless.

The sound of a stick knocking against the rocky path leading to the estate made her turn around, and wiped the smile from her face. Her great-grandfather, Jean-Claude, sunbaked and wrinkled, was hobbling painfully up the unpaved feeder road to the plot. Gemma's lips pursed. She glanced at her father and noticed his expression had turned grim and slightly weary. Jean-Claude rarely ventured out to the fields these days. They all knew an age-old argument was about to begin.

Gemma did not dislike her great-grandfather, but he was a strange man, hard to feel affection for. She had never seen him happy and could not ever remember hearing him laugh. She visited him every other day, because her mother made her. She was burdened with this duty by virtue of being his only great-grandchild. His "Legacy" as he called her. The farm's prosperity certainly brought him no joy. In fact, the more green, the more lush, the more plentiful and hardy the crop, the more discontented he seemed.

"Grand Pere," her father acknowledged.

Jean-Claude grunted in return and moved painfully past his grandson to look at the fields. He ever so slowly bent over a nearby row of lettuce, and looked it over carefully.

"It's a very good crop this year Grand Pere," her father said, "One of the best yet. Even with the dry season we didn't lose anything. The pineapples and watermelons are some of the biggest we've ever seen."

Jean-Claude made no comment. He inspected several heads of lettuce and eventually stood up, his back made a dry sounding cracking noise.

"No flowers." He replied.

Her father frowned, "Eh?"

"No yellow flowers means no seed."

Her father inhaled sharply, "Encore!" his voice raised but he controlled himself.
"Grand Pere, the Lab gives us all the seed we need. You know that. Since your time, all seed comes from them. They make the seed stronger. We get better crops."

Jean-Claude spat on the dry soil in disgust.

"Terminator seed. One crop and everything done. Every time you want to plant you have to go back to them. Is not natural! Seed supposed to come from the crop!"

Her father rubbed his face vigorously with his hand, and she knew his temper was rising.

"Grand Pere, you have to let this go. Is just the way things are now. The Lab gives us all the seed we need for the year. We never lose a crop, and we always have something to ship to the overseas market. You want us to go back to your day eh? When every little hurricane flatten the fields? What about Black Stigatoka?"

Jean-Claude visibly reeled at the mention of the dreaded pest. Her father continued on; relentlessly.

"Yes! You remember that one, eh? Your whole banana plantation destroyed because of that one! And is EverGreen coming back here that save the island from agricultural ruin!"

But Jean-Claude was not known for backing down from any fight. On the contrary, he had a reputation as a stubborn rebel.

He retorted, "Yes! But at what cost, Arthur? At what cost? Is me they come to first with their poison seed! And I let them plant and experiment. God forgive me…" He seemed to choke with intense emotion. "Is not right what they do. First is the hybrid, and then they start changing things. Bigger watermelons, sweeter pineapples, drought resistant greens…they even cure the Stigatoka. It was a miracle."

His voice trembled and trailed off into something like a sob. It was then Gemma was suddenly struck by how truly ancient he was. To her ten year-old mind, Jean-Claude was a force of nature. Now, he seemed bowed and bent with the weight of all his ninety years. By contrast, her father stood tall, strong and well -muscled, his skin glowed with vitality.

Arthur sighed heavily, "I'm sorry Grand Pere, but is enough now. Is dangerous to talk like that. I know is hard for you to understand, but farming change now. Is illegal to have heirloom seed," his voice lowered automatically, "It's better for everybody this way."

Jean-Claude stared at him from underneath white bushy eyebrows, his dark brown eyes cloudy but fierce.

"Gemma!" he called sharply.

Gemma started but then quickly jumped up and ran over to them.

"Yes Papa?" she asked nervously.

Jean-Claude grabbed her little wrist and pulled her hand up so roughly she was forced to stand on tiptoe.

He glared at Arthur and then they all stared at Gemma's misshapen hand with the little finger missing. The finger had never existed. The hand had simply formed with three fingers and a thumb.

"Not natural!" Jean-Claude hissed, "Poison seed!"

Arthur's face darkened with rage.

"Let her go old man," he ordered.

Jean-Claude let go of her wrist and with some effort calmed himself. She could see the deep, carved wrinkles at the corners of his eyes were wet.

"Sorry, Gemma. Don't forget to do your lessons, ok?" Jean-Claude's tone softened as he spoke to her. He awkwardly patted her cornrowed hair.

Gemma nodded reluctantly. She didn't like Jean-Claude's lessons. It was just endless repetition of fruits and vegetables and numbers. He made her say them over and over again and got mad if she made a mistake. She left the two men in their tense stand-off and went off reciting under her breath, "Carrots-13,000, tomatoes-23,000, lettuce-50,000…"

In the days that followed, Gemma forgot about the confrontation as she went down to the city to visit her Aunty Lisa, and her cousins Maude and Roy. The children spent their annual summer holidays together, and engaged in their favourite pastime, swimming in the bay in front of the string of luxury hotels. A few elderly, amateur fishermen from the town would come to try their luck in the bay, although they knew it was an exercise in futility. They chatted amongst themselves about bait, techniques, and all the fish their ancestors caught in past times. Fishing was now a hobby.

Many years before Gemma was born, foreign trawlers had swept through the sea of St. Marts netting schools of fish and sea life indiscriminately. Whole species simply vanished.
According to her father, fish was now grown in massive nurseries at the various EverGreen branches, island wide. This had led to another shouting match between her father and Jean-Claude over something to do with genetics.

It seemed to Gemma that Jean-Claude was always quarrelling about crimes against nature. He was angry at the Lab, at her father, at the government; at everybody it seemed. He said farmers' rights had been taken away. And then her father would say their family farm had been a Lab' success story. He had even called her his little seed, because the Lab had helped her to grow in mummy's tummy; mummy didn't like to talk about it because she said God had turned his back on the women of St. Marts.

She splashed in the clear, turquoise, salty water and then lazily raised her hand to her face. She trailed water from her fingertips. Almost all the kids she knew had four fingers. A few of her friends at school only had four toes on each foot too, and her cousin Roy had a hand that looked like a claw. Nobody really talked about it, or appeared to know why it happened. There was a zero tolerance policy in school for teasing and bullying. But now so many kids had the same type of hands it no longer mattered.

She sputtered as Roy splashed her in the face. They screamed with laughter. They dived down to the very bottom, and frolicked between the seaweed covered rocks.

At night, even though she was on vacation, Gemma lay in bed mentally going over her lessons. Instinctively, she knew what Jean-Claude was teaching her was deeply important. Beans-200,000; pigeon peas-300, 000; lettuce-50,000…

She soon drifted into a dreamless sleep.

A few days before summer vacation ended, her father called to say Papa had died. He had been buried quietly, and there had been no need to spoil Gemma's vacation with the sad news. Gemma was strangely relieved, and felt a little guilty that she wasn't as sad as Aunty Lisa who cried, and called Papa, "That poor ol' senile man". Perhaps, because she felt guilty, Gemma continued her lessons faithfully; now, at bedtime, she recited her figures twice.

On the last day of August, Gemma made her goodbyes to Aunty Lisa, and Maude and Roy and drove back with her father to their farm on Morn Fran. Driving into the village, bounty overflowed as far as the eye could see. The annual flower show was coming up, and the whole community was festooned in huge, vivid flowers; every garden equally beautiful despite the scorching heat, and with the same types of flowers.

Her father drove the black, Toyota pickup with his usual speed, making Gemma bounce up and down over the potholes on the feeder road up to the farm. They drove past a man who was walking up the steep hill with surprising ease, despite his long robes. She watched him in the side mirror and wondered how he could bear the heat with his head wrapped up in so much cloth. Papa had once said the Prophet was as old as the hills, but that was just a story, because Papa looked a lot older than him.

 She heard the sound of loose gravel hitting the undercarriage. Her father didn't say much on the journey except to say Papa was in Heaven now.

She felt a faint stirring of disquiet.

Now as they pulled up a few yards from the house, he stopped the truck. They stayed in the old vehicle, just sitting and looking at the pristine white house with its green porch and windows. Several citrus trees encircled it. Beyond, they could make out the outline of the next mountain, the stone capped Morn Pelé. Sweat began to trickle down her lean back, as the August sun beat down on the metal roof. Her father kept his hands on the steering wheel. Gemma waited.

"Gemma, did Papa ever talk to you…about the Book?" he asked at last.

Gemma caught her breath. They never spoke about the Book. The Book was never to be discussed. It was dangerous. She was not even supposed to know about it. Suddenly she could hear her own heartbeat. Her father continued talking without taking his eyes off the house.

"I want you to listen to me careful, ok? When Papa was young, he did something very bad. He and a man from the Lab, a scientist, made a book, a kind of ledger or record…you understand?"

He glanced at her, but she avoided his gaze. She kept her eyes studiously on her hands, intertwining her eight fingers.

He continued softly, "It was a seed catalogue of what they call heirloom stock, or original stock. The kind of plants that used to grow in St. Marts many ages ago."

He took hold of Gemma's small chin and turned her to look at him. Gemma breathed through her mouth shallowly.

"The plants we had before were bad, Gemma. They got sick and insects ate them. They were small and weak. When they died, things got very bad for everybody, food was scarce. You understand?" His fingers tightened and Gemma nodded quickly. He let go of her chin but held her gaze intently.

"Papa and the scientist should not have made that Book. It was illegal to have that kind of seed. The police put Papa in Stockfarm for over a year."

Gemma's lips trembled. She knew of course. Aunty Lisa was always talking about the shame on the George family name, because Papa had been in prison. Hearing it from her father, however, made it real and terrible.

She wanted to ask why Papa had to go to prison because of a book. She wanted to ask why some seeds were so bad, and yet other seeds so important. She wanted to go into the house and hug her mother, and never ask such questions.

"The police think Papa hid some original seed, and the Book tells where he hid it. They ...tried to make him talk but he never confessed. The Swiss scientist got away for a while and he was hiding in the heights when they caught him."

He stopped, leaving the fate of the mysterious scientist forever unknown.

Gemma looked longingly and desperately at the house, with its white walls and lime green veranda and windows.

"Did Papa tell you about the Book, Gemma?" His voice was low, urgent.

"No Daddy," Gemma answered truthfully.

His deep sigh filled the cab of the truck.

"I am the Book." Her small voice was as loud and clear as a bell.

Her father's ebony skin turned ashen. His mouth dropped open. Tears rolled down her cheeks as she began tonelessly to recite what Jean Claude had taught her for years.

"Carrots-13,000, tomatoes-23,000, lettuce-50,000 Beans-200,000, pigeon peas-300,000, lettuce-50,000..."

He clapped his large hand over her mouth and scanned the area around them. Of course there was no one there. He quickly dropped his hand, turned on the ignition and rolled up the windows. Leaving the motor idling he turned on the air condition, and then paused from this flurry of activity to stare at her. The sun disappeared behind the clouds giving much needed respite from the glare.

Gemma could not seem to stop herself from talking. She recited the whole catalogue, even correcting herself when she made a mistake. Papa was wrong to have made a bad book, and then make her learn it. Daddy said so.

The last things she said made even less sense to her, than the fruits and vegetables and numbers. These were numbers too but Papa had tried to teach her to say, latitude and longitude before them. They were very hard words, so she just said "lat and long" instead. Her father reacted when she said them.

"That's here, up in the heights …" he whispered to himself, "A cave or someplace dry and cold. They would have needed somewhere dark…and safe. Enough seed to start the farm over…" He seemed to forget she was there.

The sun came out from behind the clouds, and Gemma looked at their home gleaming in the bright light. The fields of emerald plants also glistened with promise, rows upon rows in the distance.

Her father gazed at the glorious green ahead and saw them for they really were; plants with no seeds. But in a cave somewhere on the mountain, an untainted future could be theirs. He took her small hand in his rough calloused one, and stared at her four fingers for a long time.

"What else did Papa tell you?" he whispered.

"He said when I grow up, I must teach it to my children, and they must teach their children. He said everybody is going to get very sick because all the food we grow is bad."

She looked at him anxiously, and he managed to give a reassuring nod.

"Papa said one day it will be safe, and then we have to go find it, to make the island special again."

Gemma was vague on what "it" was exactly, but it must be a treasure she surmised. She was relieved to see her father did not seem angry; just resigned in his expression. She worried if perhaps, the police would come to take her to Stockfarm now. Gemma, completely exhausted and feeling strangely empty, asked, "Daddy, can we go home now?"

He looked once more at her little hands and decided they were too small for their burden.

"Yes love, and at bedtime, I want you to teach me too."

The End

Printed in Great Britain
by Amazon